BUYING A RETIREMENT HOME

Jack P. Friedman, PhD, CPA
Senior Manager, the Roulac Group
Deloitte & Touche, Dallas, Texas

Jack C. Harris, PhD
Real Estate Center
Texas A&M University
College Station, Texas

BARRON'S

New York • London • Toronto • Sydney

All inquiries should be addressed to:
Barron's Educational Series, Inc.
250 Wireless Boulevard
Hauppauge, New York 11788

Library of Congress Catalog Card Number 90-24716

International Standard Book No. 0-8120-4476-2

Library of Congress Cataloging-in-Publication Data
Friedman, Jack P.
Keys to buying a retirement home / Jack P. Friedman, Jack C. Harris.
p. cm. — (Barron's retirement keys)
Includes index.
ISBN 0-8120-4476-2
1. House buying. 2. Retirees—Housing. 3. Aged—Dwellings.
4. Retirement communities. 5. Life care communities. I. Harris,
Jack C., 1945- . II. Title. III. Series.
HD1390.5.F74 1991
362.1'6—dc20 90-24716
CIP

PRINTED IN THE UNITED STATES OF AMERICA
1234 5500 987654321

CONTENTS

Section III—Semi-Independent Living

Section IV—Dependent Living

Section V— Financial Considerations

INTRODUCTION

Living in suitable housing is a matter that everyone faces. We seek housing that is appropriate from several standpoints, including its physical characteristics, social setting, and affordability. Housing considerations change upon retirement. For example, instead of seeking to satisfy your children's needs as when you bought your first home, you can focus on your own needs, which are now quite different because of your age. This doesn't mean that you need to go through the trauma of moving—your present housing and neighborhood may be perfectly satisfactory. But, some factors to consider include access to shopping, transportation, and health care facilities. And amenities inside your home may need change, with possibilities ranging from a cosmetic improvement (repainting with a brighter color) to a major renovation.

The purpose of this book is to describe the array of housing that is available to the retired. More importantly, it offers insights into key elements needed to make an appropriate housing decision.

Taking stock of your present situation is one of the first things you will wish to do. Keys 1 through 11 discuss your current housing situation, personal state of health, preferred lifestyle, and finances.

Keys 12 through 27 focus on choices that are available for people who need not depend on anyone else for care. It provides information on a wide array of possible housing arrangements, and financing patterns that are especially useful or specifically designed for the retired.

Keys 28 through 33 describe housing options for semi-independent people, who are those that regularly need a helping hand from a care-giving person. Housing choices are more limited than for the independent.

Keys 34 through 37 describe options for those who are dependent on others for basic care. Dependent people need close supervision and continuous help with daily functions. They have housing options, though they are the most limited group.

Keys 38 through 46 provide information on financial considerations, particularly those related to housing. Key issues include federal, state, and local programs for the elderly, as well as financial matters with no government participation.

Housing selection for the retired and elderly is not a cut-and-dried matter. Rather, it depends as much on an individual's psychological and emotional needs as it does on the person's physical capabilities. We sincerely hope that readers benefit by making a better informed decision that will meet their housing needs.

Jack Friedman
Jack Harris

1

ASSESSING THE LEVEL OF SUPPORT NEEDED

Retirement housing is more than just a question of shelter. The housing decision involves a whole array of support services necessary for comfort and security. Determining just how much support you need depends on your physical and mental condition at the time. Now that people are living for long periods after retirement age, housing needs can change several times during retirement.

The main consideration in choosing the appropriate type of housing is how dependent the retiree is on outside help. Those who are as physically, mentally, and socially independent as when they were younger need no special arrangement. Many can remain in the homes they have occupied for many years, whereas some choose to travel or enjoy a warmer or drier climate. At the opposite end of the scale are those who require constant medical monitoring and assistance with basic bodily functions. Their needs are complex, extensive, and ever present. There are many degrees of independence between these two extremes.

It might be helpful to divide retirement situations into three categories. If you can place your situation or that of your retired relative in one of these categories, you can begin to settle on the type of housing needed.

The **totally independent** retiree is one who remains active physically with only minor impairment in mobility. No assistance is needed in getting places, taking meals, or tending to personal hygiene. The person is mentally alert and capable of making rational decisions.

There is no chronic illness or medical condition that might require extraordinary emergency access. Both spouses are still present or the person is active socially.

The **semi-independent** retiree suffers some impairment in mobility that requires special equipment or design features. For example, a wheelchair or walker may be necessary. Some help may be needed to eat, dress, or use the bathroom. The person may have some medical condition that needs periodic attention and should have access to emergency medical assistance. He or she may not be as mentally attentive as when younger. The person may be widowed and without regular social interaction with family or friends.

The **totally dependent** person has suffered a major decline of physical or mental capability. This person requires constant assistance and monitoring and is totally incapable of performing the basic functions of life unassisted.

In subsequent keys, other considerations will be discussed. Later sections of the book will review the major options for housing based on these considerations.

2

TAKING STOCK OF YOUR RESOURCES

The personal resources you have accumulated throughout your life will determine much of your retirement living options. Therefore, a first step in your planning is to figure out what these resources are. Consider resources in a rather broad sense, including sources of retirement income, your home and possessions, and relatives and other personal relationships.

Your income during retirement will consist of income from personal savings, Social Security benefits, any pension rights you may have, and, possibly, income from part-time work. You should make an accounting to see how much these sources will provide on a sustainable basis. Although the combined total may not equal your income during your working years, in most cases you will not need as much income in retirement because you will not have work-related expenses and have less need to accumulate savings for the future.

Income from personal savings is an important component of retirement planning. You may want to rearrange the assets in your portfolio to better match the unique requirements of retirement life. First, you probably will want to assure that the portfolio provides a substantial amount of current income. However, don't neglect some capital growth needs. You will need to counter erosion of capital from inflation. In addition, you will need some liquidity (quick access to cash) in case of an emergency.

Incredibly, some people have old savings accounts, savings bonds, or stocks that they have forgotten. You may want to go back over old tax returns to make sure you haven't overlooked some of these hidden assets. This also may be the time to make withdrawals from your IRA, Keogh, or other tax-deferred savings. The rules are complex, so you may want to hire a financial planner to help do this.

Social Security income should be considered. If you held a job covered by the program, you may be entitled to benefits at the established retirement age. Contact your local Social Security office to check on your eligibility and benefits. Surviving spouses of workers covered by the program also are eligible for benefits. In addition, there are benefits for disabled workers that can be obtained before retirement age.

You also should figure out what you can expect from any pensions that you may have. Pension programs generally operate in one of two ways. You may be entitled to a *defined benefit,* related to how many years you worked for the company and what your salary was. Defined benefit programs generally provide a certain amount of income for the remainder of your lifetime. The other method calls for a *defined contribution* by which a certain amount of money is invested each period, often in assets of your choice. In this case, you have an account from which you may withdraw funds until the account is depleted. If you worked for the company long enough to be vested, you are entitled to the company's contribution in addition to the money you put in. Be sure to check on past jobs you may have held to see if you still have any benefits coming.

If you own a home, it can be a major resource for retirement planning. A home is a major asset that can be turned into cash. It also may be adapted to suit your needs, should you decide not to move. Also consider possessions that may be sold for additional cash. This may be the time to sell works of art or antiques you may have accumulated for their investment value.

Finally, consider the personal relationships that may help in your retirement planning. Would it be possible to move in with your children, if need be? Would it be desirable? Do you have close friends with whom you might want to consolidate households? Whereas finances are important, social relationships are equally important to a satisfactory life during retirement.

3

LIVING COSTS

The various options available to you in retirement involve different levels of costs. In this regard, we refer to the continuing costs of living that must be covered by your sources of income and other types of assistance (such as insurance programs and special Social Security benefits). One of the problems faced by most retirees is that of inflation. In many cases, income from savings and pensions is either fixed or imperfectly related to general inflation. Unless you design some allowance for rising costs into your plans, you may suffer from increasing depletion of funds or a declining living standard over time.

There is much you can do to try to align living costs with your anticipated retirement income. If you are totally independent (see Key 1), your decision to move or stay put will determine your level of costs. For those who are dependent to some extent, the level of professional services used will dictate costs.

First, let's look at the move-stay decision. If you expect that your retirement income will support your present standard of living, you may wish to stay in your present home or move to another home of comparable costs (possibly to a more desirable location). If you don't think you can afford your present home, you have several alternatives. One would be to decrease expenses by paying off the mortgage on the home. This is attractive especially when your mortgage interest rate is high or you cannot benefit much from the tax deductibility of mortgage interest.

Another way to reduce expenses is finding someone

to move in with you and share costs. You also could reduce your costs by moving to a less expensive home. Or you could do both by selling the home, putting the proceeds into an annuity providing periodic income, and renting a less expensive home. If you expect that you will have more than enough to support your current lifestyle, you may want to trade up to a more luxurious home (not necessarily larger) or move to a resort development.

If you require some type of physical or medical assistance, your cost depends on the level of professional services needed. The amount of assistance you receive may not be something that you can control. However, you may satisfy your needs with help from relatives or friends, or by entering some type of publicly-provided institution or a private, highly-specialized facility. Obviously, the level you can afford will determine the convenience and reliability of service. The important point to remember is that there is some discretion available even when your need for assistance is out of your hands.

Consider that your financial needs will not be uniform during your retirement. Think of the rest of your life as composed of several stages. From now until you actually retire, you will be making arrangements for a successful retirement. As the time approaches, make every effort to reduce debts and gain financial flexibility. Early retirement may involve a transition period when your spouse continues working or you do some part-time work. You will have additional income but also some work-related expenses. The next period is one of complete retirement, meaning reduced income but lower expenses. Finally, there may be a time of partial or complete infirmity that will require you to call upon your financial resources to their fullest.

4

TO MOVE OR STAY PUT

In many ways, it is natural to think of moving when you retire. Because your daily existence will be different, you may find the home you occupied when working not to be ideal or even appropriate. It commonly is thought that older people feel burdened by a house that is too large for their current needs. That is one reason Congress enacted the $125,000 exemption of gain from income tax for those over age 55 who sell their principal residence (see Key 45).

The reality is that people rarely move when they retire. A 1987 survey conducted by the Harvard-MIT Joint Center for Housing Studies found that only 20 percent of those over age 55 had moved. Only five percent stated that they planned to move in the next five years and this figure declined to one percent for those over age 65. The vast majority were content to stay in their existing homes, and the very oldest have the deepest roots with very few having any intention of moving. Surprisingly, very few respondents to the survey felt the house was too large or that they had more space than they could use.

There is no compelling reason to move when you retire unless you find your current surroundings unsatisfactory. Here are some of the things that might make you consider a move:

- The home is too costly to maintain. You still may have mortgage payments that cut into retirement income (check to see if you can pay off the loan at some discount). The house may need major repairs or constant maintenance because of its age. It may be that it simply is too much trouble to keep clean.

- The design of the house makes it difficult for you to get around. If the home has stairways or an inefficient floor plan, these may become bigger problems as you become less agile. If you need a wheelchair, a stairway may make part of the home inaccessible altogether.
- The neighborhood has changed over the years and you no longer feel safe, or your old friends have moved away.

Your home environment can be much more important in retirement than when you were working. Consider that you probably will spend much more time in the home. Having convenient shopping, recreational facilities, and friends close by will become more essential. Within the bounds of your available resources, you may as well make your home as comfortable and supportive as possible.

You also should consider that the longer you delay moving, the more difficult it will be. Aside from the physical problems of packing up everything and carting it off to a new location, the psychological effects of moving increase with age. It is hard especially when someone has lived in a home for a long time. There may be a great many fond memories associated with the house and the neighborhood. A move can instill a real feeling of loss when the focus of these memories is removed. Therefore, if you still live in the old family house, you will want to give much thought to how willing you are to part with it.

The keys that follow will cover many of the aspects of the home environment that you should consider in your decision to move or stay. In each case, evaluate how important that aspect is to you, what you plan to do with the rest of your life, and how well that particular need is satisfied by your current surroundings.

5

SPACE NEEDS

Roominess is one of the most important characteristics of a home. In general, people are willing to pay more for additional space, up to a limit. However, you may find your need for spacious quarters changes as you age.

A popular misconception about housing is that older people are eager to unload their current homes because they find them too big for their needs. Actually, surveys have discovered that more people move into larger homes after they retire than those who trade for smaller homes. Some people find that when they finally have taken care of most of their financial obligations, they finally can afford the kind of home they always dreamed of. They indulge their desires for luxuries and room.

Nevertheless, more space is not an unqualified benefit. Larger homes are more expensive to purchase and to maintain. Therefore, you should make a critical evaluation of how much space you really need as part of your housing decision process. Look at your current space from the standpoint of what is usable. Your home may have whole rooms that are used infrequently because they don't fit well into the floor plan (a bedroom without convenient access to a bath or without good ventilation) or are too inaccessible (a basement den that requires frequent climbing of stairs). For your current home and any new one you are considering moving to, identify how much space is relatively unusable. Consider that your tolerance of inconvenience will diminish as you get older, so be rather picky in your evaluation.

Next consider your needs for the following kinds of

space. Room will be more important if you require assistance in getting around. Hallways and doors may need to be wider to accommodate a wheelchair, and steps will present a barrier. If you have children or close friends, you may want to maintain a guest room to encourage visits. This room also could double as a place to display collectibles or as a small library.

Don't shortchange yourself on space for activities you enjoy. Outside space is important if you like to grow things (as well as some type of place for propagating seeds). You'll need space for your pets. When you retire, hobbies can take on new importance in satisfying your need to be productive. Finally, consider how space can promote a sense of privacy. Usually smaller homes mean you live closer to your neighbors. For some, this is desirable, especially if they share interests with neighbors. However, many others find such a situation uncomfortable.

You may not be able to meet your space desires on a limited budget. Once you know what you would like, you can cut back if need be to fit what you can afford.

6

LIFESTYLE CONSIDERATIONS

For your home life to be satisfactory, your home should fit the way you want to live. You can find a home that physically meets your needs, but it is as important to make sure that it enables you to do the things you want to do and represents the type of values you desire.

Lifestyle considerations will take on new importance after you retire. Because you will not be spending a large part of your day on a job site, you will need to find more satisfaction from your home environment. Also, you may find that you can't move around town as easily as you once did and will be less tolerant of inconveniences and irritations at home. You should take special pains to minimize such problems.

Consider what you plan to do with your time after retirement. If you will spend time on hobbies and crafts, you will want space devoted to those activities. If you expect to travel, you may want to reduce your responsibilities for the upkeep of your home, or you may desire some type of security that will give you peace of mind when you are away.

Location also is important to supporting your desired lifestyle. You may want to be closer to family and friends. If you are contemplating moving in with family or sharing quarters with a friend, make sure that the arrangement does not compromise whatever privacy and control of your time that you want. Consider places you will go to on a routine basis and try to make your access to these places as convenient as possible.

One of the worst destroyers of a satisfactory home

life is conflict and interference by those living around you. You may desire to live in a smaller home to reduce housekeeping responsibilities. If that means living with people whom you don't like or are incompatible with, the trade-off may not be worthwhile. If you are considering renting or moving into a condominium, pay special attention to your future neighbors and the way they live. It is inevitable that you will be affected if your lifestyle is significantly different from your close neighbors. Living in such arrangements means sharing space, and calls for compromises on everyone's part in how those areas are used. Make sure you can live with those compromises.

Like all the considerations discussed in this book, lifestyle should be one factor in forming an idea of your ideal retirement home. Recognize that you may have to economize on your ideal in light of your available finances and physical capabilities. You may have to compromise to arrange something affordable, but don't neglect or shortchange your lifestyle needs.

7

NEED FOR PRIVACY

The human need for privacy is fundamental to the housing choice. All of us want some space and time to ourselves, yet people crave social contact. That's why most people like living in a detached home with its own yard that is surrounded by congenial neighbors. This arrangement provides the right amount of privacy and social interaction for the majority.

That desired mix may change as we age. When it gets harder to get about, it is nice to have friends and acquaintances (and possibly relatives) closer by. If we feel more vulnerable to the world around us, we may feel more secure by having neighbors within shouting distance. A greater need for emergency medical assistance heightens our desire for nearby friends. When a spouse is lost, these concerns are even greater. Therefore, when choosing retirement housing, consider how much privacy you are willing to give up for the advantages of more accessible neighbors.

How you fit in the dependency categories discussed in Key 1 will determine much of your decision. Obviously, the more dependent you are, the less privacy you can afford. For example, assuming that you are independent upon retirement, you can attain maximum privacy in your own home. By contrast, a nursing home offers little privacy, extensive potential social contact, as well as constant observation by the professional staff.

Many retired people find a good compromise by living in condominium or rental housing. Depending on the size and design of your unit, you can enjoy the privacy of an individual housing unit. At the same time, the buffer between you and your neighbors is much smaller, possibly only a hallway or party wall. Outdoor activities are conducted in an area generally shared with other residents of the complex. As long as you remain compatible with your neighbors, this arrangement can provide benefits. Increasingly, condominium and rental complexes are being developed that cater to the needs of retirees and may even restrict entry to those under a specified age. And, of course, many retirees spent their entire lives in apartment units and are most comfortable continuing in that arrangement.

Privacy is closely related to lifestyle (Key 6) and space (Key 5) considerations. The ideal is to have enough privacy to do those things you prefer to do alone or in selected company, but with access to neighbors and friends as convenient as possible.

8

THE RIGHT LOCATION

When you selected your current home, you probably paid a good deal of attention to where it was located. You wanted a place that was not too far away from where you work and reasonably convenient to shopping and other points of interest. You may have even based much of your decision on proximity to good quality schools for your children.

When you choose a place to retire, location is no less important. But you will have a different set of considerations from those you had when you were younger. Some of the places you needed to be near before no longer will be important. Other places will be more important. In addition, how you get to these places may change, meaning that access to public transportation could be an essential factor.

Older age could mean more frequent visits to a doctor. Convenience in getting to and from a doctor's office, as well as a good source of emergency medical aid, should be considered. If you have family in town, you may wish to live close by.

Some people even move long distances to be in the same town as their children. Other places you frequented in the past will continue to be important. These include shopping areas, recreational areas (such as your favorite fishing hole), and religious and cultural institutions.

Consider that, as you age, your ability to travel may be impaired. Living too far from some favored place of interest may mean you rarely get a chance to visit. It may be worthwhile to sit down and list the places you enjoy and try to rank them in order of how often you make the trip and how important it is to continue to visit.

There probably is no location that will provide ideal proximity to all the places you want to go. You may find that some things you used to go out for can be delivered to your home. The occasional evening at a restaurant may be replaced with home delivered pizza or Chinese food. You may even find a grocery that delivers, and the delivery charge and/or tip is a worthwhile price for the service.

Retirement communities usually are arranged so that everything is within easy access to residents. There are even recreational and social programs designed for retirees. But, they can't provide for close proximity to family and friends. So if frequent contact with them is important, you may want to forgo the convenience of the community.

9

NEIGHBORHOOD SAFETY

It is a sad fact that many of our older city neighborhoods no longer are safe places to be. This especially is a problem for older people who feel some attachment to their longtime neighborhood. What may have once been a thriving area of home owners may now be a transitional neighborhood in which youth gangs prey upon the defenseless. Living in such an area may cause you to feel even more isolated and alone.

A fundamental change in neighborhood quality is one important reason you may wish to relocate. Obviously, it will do no good to move into a situation that is just as bad. Therefore, spend some effort in checking out the new neighborhood.

If you are planning on buying a home, look for an area where most everyone is a home owner. If you don't know someone in the area to ask, look for signs of people taking pride in their homes, such as good lawn and property maintenance. Avoid any area where homes are noticeably deteriorating.

Look for evidence of good public services. Is the neighborhood kept clean? Are streets and sidewalks in good repair? There should be regular police patrols. But, too conspicuous presence of police may indicate that the area is a center of crime. Parks and open space are desirable in a residential neighborhood. Too often, however, they are locations where criminals and vagrants congregate. If you are looking at an area with public parks, ask local residents about them.

Many retirement communities have their own security systems. Generally, there is limited access to the village and there are full-time guards to check who goes in and out. In addition, residents will have passed some type of screening. If security is a major concern, you may want to consider this option.

10

DESIGN FOR RETIREMENT LIVING

Real estate agents will tell you that a good floor plan can add value to a home. When you spend as much time in your home as you do, you want it to be as convenient as possible. Features that detract from convenience and make doing routine tasks more difficult can be tolerated when you are young. For many older people, these detractions can become obstacles and limit their ability to do many routine and necessary things.

When you are young, a multi-story home can have some advantages. An upstairs bedroom or basement den provides a place to retreat from the bustle of family life. However, when climbing stairs requires extraordinary physical effort or is prohibited by some disability, remote areas of the home become less useful. Equipment is available to overcome these obstacles, such as special wheelchair lifts that can be retrofitted onto conventional stairways, if you wish to go to the expense. Generally, a single-story home is preferable.

When looking at a new home, consider your daily activities and how easily they could be conducted in the space. If you need aids to get around, make sure there is enough room for such equipment in doorways and other passages. Pay special attention to the kitchen and baths, where so much daily routine occurs. You will want to minimize unnecessary trips and movement in doing these tasks.

Another important consideration is the difficulty in cleaning and maintenance. Choose easy-to-maintain materials, if possible. This is important especially for interior space. It is easier to hire people to keep your lawn and grounds in shape than to hire maid service. Often, the less space you have to maintain the better, especially if much of that space is not useful to you on a regular basis.

Given this emphasis on convenience, you may also want to include features that make it inviting and pleasurable to get moderate exercise. Physical activity still is valuable regardless of your age or physical limitations. You are less likely to engage in any exercise if it is difficult to get started. Some of the features that may help are a backyard lap pool, access to a pleasant wooded area for taking walks or any outdoor area where you can enjoy leisure sports (such as croquet or shuffleboard). Many excellent exercise facilities are available in condominium or rental apartment complexes. Check to see how these facilities are used and how crowded they become. You may find you will avoid their use if they are filled with young children or simply rarely available.

11

CHOOSING YOUR RETIREMENT HOME

The preceding keys describe the basic factors you should consider when deciding where to spend your retirement. All this information can be confusing until you develop a strategy for making that decision. This key offers one such strategy.

To begin, you must make some basic decisions that will determine the type of place most suitable to your situation. First, you must decide how much medical and social support you will need—whether you are independent of regular assistance, somewhat dependent, or totally dependent. Second, you will need to decide whether you care to move from your current home or try to create a satisfactory environment where you are. Third, you must evaluate the financial resources you can access to arrange your choice. The remaining keys in this book provide information on most of the options you have to choose from. The chart below is a guide to those keys based on your answers to the basic questions we have discussed.

	LEVEL OF SUPPORT NEEDED		
	Independent	**Semi-Dependent**	**Totally Dependent**
Decision not to move:	Sale lease-back (16) Equity conversion (14, 15) Home sharing (13) Remodeling (12)	Adult day care (32) Professional home care (28) Medical remodeling (30)	Foster care (34)

Decision to move:	Subsidized housing (26)	Living with family (29)	Nursing homes (36)
	Trading down (17, 18, 19)	Caring for a parent (35)	
	Co-purchase (21)	Congregate housing (33)	
	Transient living (24)	Senior citizen centers (31)	
	Retirement communities (23)		
	Resort living (22)		

Notice that the options diminish as your need for support increases. When making a decision that requires a sizable investment, consider that your need for support may vary over time. Therefore, the decision you make now may not cover your entire retirement.

Once you have made a basic decision on the type of housing most suitable, you can evaluate specific places in light of other considerations. For each prospective choice, consider the following:

- How much privacy you require in your daily life.
- The type of lifestyle you intend to pursue.
- Your requirements for both interior and outdoor space.
- The most desirable location relative to places you frequent.
- Your personal security.
- Design features that add convenience and utility to your daily life.

Rarely will people be able to obtain a home that fits their ideal perfectly. In all likelihood, you will have to make some compromises, particularly if your situation is relatively inflexible. By using these considerations to make those trade-offs, you should be able to put together the best mix of features for an enjoyable retirement.

12

REMODELING YOUR PRESENT HOME

If you don't wish to move, but your current home doesn't exactly fit your needs, consider remodeling. Within limits, you may be able to make your current home come reasonably close to your ideal. Remodeling can be expensive, but you save the costs of moving, searching for a new home, and going through the process of buying and selling.

Before you decide to remodel, consider a few basic facts. First, most of the changes you will make to your home will be unique to your needs and desires and probably will not appeal to a prospective buyer when you are ready to sell. That means you won't recoup much of your investment if and when you sell. If you expect to make major changes, plan to stay in the house for a good while.

Second, the one thing you can't change is the location of your home. If you are too far from someplace important to you or if the neighborhood is not to your liking, remodeling is not an alternative to moving. Third, some design features can't be overcome by remodeling. For example, the inconvenience of a two-story home can be lessened but not eliminated totally. Consider remodeling only if the benefits of staying in your home greatly outweigh the drawbacks.

Here are some examples of things you may want to do. If the home is just too big for you to handle, you may want to convert some of the space to a separate dwelling unit and invite another person to use it. Check local ordinances to make sure you legally can do this.

(See Keys 25, Apartment Conversion and Key 13, Home Sharing.)

Much of the space you have may be designed for the wrong use. Changing bedrooms into space for recreation or other interests can be done with minimal expense. Costly items include remodeling a kitchen to make it easier to use and the addition of a bath for greater convenience. A general remodeling to remove obstacles or hazardous features can be done. This may include adding handrails throughout the home and replacing steps with ramps at various entryways.

Always consider ways to brighten the home. More light and brighter colors will provide a psychological lift and help prevent a growing feeling of isolation. Also, the more attractive your home, the better you will feel about yourself and the more likely you will be to invite friends and relatives to visit.

Any major program of home improvement probably will require some financing. You will find contractors and material suppliers willing to provide some financing. But, there may be lower- cost alternatives. Check local banks and savings and loans for the cost of home improvement loans. Also compare the cost of obtaining a home equity loan line of credit (Key 14). The interest rate on this type of loan usually is low because you must pledge your home as collateral. You must recognize that if you fail to pay back the loan, you could lose your home. If that bothers you, check on the costs of unsecured signature loans, particularly if the amount of the loan is not large.

When you hire people to do the remodeling work, obtain and check out their references. Unfortunately, there are unscrupulous people who pretend to be home repair contractors. They will not be able to provide references that are verifiable. Contact your local Better Business Bureau about any contractors you plan to use.

Many contractors are members of an association, such as Associated General Contractors of America, (202) 393-2040, or Associated Builders and Contractors, Inc., (202) 637-8800. Membership does not assure that the contractor has a good reputation, though it may indicate some commitment to the trade.

Find out how long they have been in business in your area—hopefully it will have been five years or longer. Do they have an office? This is an important sign of being established and may offer a telephone number to leave a message, while the work is being done or after completion to note a problem.

Ask about any guarantee they may offer. If possible, get a written estimate with some assurance the final costs will be close to the estimated amount.

13

HOME SHARING PROGRAMS

Montgomery County, Maryland, a local community in the Washington, D.C. area, offers a program that helps elderly home owners find tenants or boarders to share their homes. The program matches people willing to share their homes with others who wish to live within such an arrangement. The ideal owner is someone who has lost a spouse and still has a home that is too large for his or her needs. The tenant may be a retired person who is forced to move or needs to move but wants to stay in the same neighborhood. Program organizers make a special effort to arrange compatible matches.

The arrangement between home owner and tenant is flexible. The tenant may pay rent in cash or barter services in return for sharing the home. The home owner retains the option to terminate the relationship if it is not satisfactory. In most cases, there is no need for modification of the home to accommodate the arrangement.

If this sounds appealing to you, but you don't live in an area where such a program is organized, you may be able to emulate the program on your own. You may know someone who needs to move who, you think, would be a pleasant housemate. You might inquire through your church or social organization about possible tenants. In most cases, it probably would not be advisable to advertise publicly for someone interested in sharing your home. The problem of screening candidates may be more than you want to take on.

Once you find someone, you can negotiate the terms of the arrangement. Although not totally necessary, it would be preferable to set these terms in writing. This will reduce the possibility of misunderstandings later on. Try to cover as many contingencies as possible, such as how to terminate the arrangement, any division of duties or responsibilities, and the extent of the tenant's right to use various parts of the home.

Home sharing can be a solution to a housing problem for both the home owner and tenant.

14

HOME EQUITY LOANS

When they get ready to retire, many people find themselves "house rich but cash poor." This means that almost all of their personal wealth is tied up in their home. They may have a nice home that is more than enough for their needs, but can afford little else.

If your situation is similar, there are ways to convert the equity in your home into cash. *Equity* is the value of your home minus the mortgage debt that is owed on it. Of course, if you sell your home you will have a sizable amount of cash from its sale. But if you stay, there is no sale to provide the money.

Even if you stay in your current home, you can take some of your equity out through refinancing. For example, a home that is worth $200,000 with a mortgage of $20,000 remaining could be refinanced with a new $140,000 first mortgage loan. After retiring the old mortgage, the home owner has $120,000 in cash proceeds, minus transaction costs. Transaction costs include discount points on the new loan, a survey, a title insurance policy, a credit report, an appraisal report, loan origination fee, and possibly a prepayment fee on the original mortgage. Though these can be substantial, you still will receive cash for the bulk of the additional debt. Borrowing normally is not a taxable event, so you won't have to pay income taxes on the cash you receive.

On the other hand, suppose the home has a much greater existing debt of $120,000. You as owner could arrange a home equity loan for $20,000. Home equity loan is a nice way of referring to a second mortgage loan, which often is available as a line of credit. For example, a bank offers a credit line up to $20,000, which you can take down all at once or a little at a time by writing special checks. By contrast, a straight second mortgage provides a lump sum of money, then requires repayment of predictable amounts each month. Your preference may depend on whether you need all the money at once (for home remodeling, for example) and are willing to accept uncertain repayment requirements.

In either case, the loan provides a way to get cash out of your home when you already have a mortgage and do not want to, or cannot, refinance the old loan for some reason. One reason would be that the old loan has a low rate of interest.

The proceeds from the loan can be used for any purpose you choose. It doesn't have to be reinvested in the home. No matter what you use the money for, interest you pay is an itemized deduction on your federal income taxes. In fact, any debt you add to your home, up to $100,000 more than the cost of remodeling and improvements, will generate tax-deductible interest expense.

Home equity loans are available from most banks and savings and loans, as well as finance companies and many investment firms. Many lenders hold closing costs to a nominal amount as a way of attracting business in this competitive field. Although the loans are second mortgages, interest rates may be only slightly above first mortgage loans. There are other costs involved, including an appraisal, survey, credit check, loan origination and loan discount, title and legal fees, and so on. If you are interested in a home equity loan, refer to Barron's *Keys to Mortgage Financing and Refinancing* for more details.

There are several things you should keep in mind about refinancing and home equity loans. Recognize that the proceeds from these loans represent debt, not income. You do have to pay the loan back. It is best to use the proceeds for special expenses that would be difficult or impossible to pay in cash. For example, a home equity loan might be used to pay large medical expenses or for home remodeling. These loans do not provide supplemental income unless the proceeds can be invested at a much higher yield than the interest on the loan.

Most home equity lines of credit have variable interest rates. If interest rates go up in the economy, the cost of the loan may go up as well. The rate on the loan is tied to a specified index that tends to reflect market interest rates. Repaying such a loan could be a problem for someone on a fixed income, especially if interest rates increase.

Finally, by using your home to support the loan, you are offering the lender the right to take your home if you fail to pay the loan. This right should not be granted casually. You may be house rich now, but failure to use mortgage credit wisely could leave you with no home at all.

15

REVERSE ANNUITY MORTGAGES

To provide extra income for retirement, you can convert to cash the equity you own in your home. One way to do this is to sell the home and move. If you don't want to move, you can mortgage the property to obtain a loan. With a new first mortgage, second mortgage, or home equity loan, you must make monthly loan payments. A reverse annuity loan, by contrast, relieves you of monthly payments, and you can use the proceeds as supplemental income.

Here's how such a loan works. You own a home free and clear or with a large amount of equity. (To find out how much equity you have, you need an estimate of your home's value. Equity is the difference between market value and the amount you owe on any mortgage loans on the house.) You take out a reverse annuity mortgage, pledging the home as collateral. The lender will pay you a specified sum according to the type of payout option you choose. All outstanding principal (the amount you borrow) and interest earned by your lender are allowed to accumulate in an account. The loan is repaid when you move or sell the home, or from your estate after your death. In a way, it is like selling your home a little at a time, although the lender gains only a claim against its value, never title to the property.

There are a great number of variations in the way cash from the loan may be borrowed. The three basic choices are one lump sum cash receipt at closing, a regular stream of cash over time, and a line of credit that allows the borrower to draw cash whenever needed. In addition, some plans allow you to combine all three types of payout. For example, you may get a portion of the cash immediately to pay closing costs (or to pay off an existing loan), set up a monthly income supplement program, and retain the right to draw on the loan whenever you need emergency cash. The monthly income plan may be based on a fixed term so that the amount of the payment can be determined. On the other hand, when the loan is insured (by the Federal Housing Administration or a private firm), payments may be arranged to last as long as you live in the home.

The FHA offers insured loans with much flexibility in terms. The cost of the insurance is a one-time premium equal to 2 percent of the loan balance plus a monthly premium. The premiums may be included in the amount that you borrow. The amount of the home's value that can be used for a FHA-insured loan is limited to the maximum FHA loan amount in your locality. If your home is worth more than the FHA maximum (up to $100,250 in some areas), you can arrange for a higher loan with a private plan.

Non-FHA loans offer both fixed-term and annuity plans. A fixed-term loan pays out until the end of a predetermined period, at which time the borrower must sell the home. If the borrower dies or moves prior to the end of the term, the loan is paid off at that time. These plans offer higher monthly income but are not available widely. Lenders are uncomfortable with the prospect of forcing home owners to move if they outlive the term of the loan. More popular are the annuity-type plans that offer benefits over the borrower's lifetime. Depending on the borrower's age, these plans provide less income than comparable fixed-term plans, because the income stream is based on the expected remaining lifetime of the borrower. These plans usually require insurance coverage paid for by the borrower.

To choose a plan, first decide on what type of income assistance you need. You may want a one-time loan to pay for remodeling your home. Or you might use a monthly income supplement to pay regular medical bills or other necessities. An annual payment could help you meet infrequent but foreseeable expenses. A line of credit could be set up for unexpected expenses. Also decide on just how much you need, either in a lump sum or periodically.

Find out your equity by getting an estimate of your home's value and subtracting the amount you owe on the home. You probably will have to pay off the old loan from the proceeds of the reverse annuity loan, so figure that expense in as a lump sum amount at closing. The more equity you have, the more beneficial the program. Also decide if you want to retain some equity at the end of the loan term. Some plans allow you to set a limit so all of your equity is not used up. Of course, any equity pledged to repay the loan will not be available to you if you sell, nor will it be a part of your estate passed on to your heirs.

If you are setting up an annuity plan, the expected term of benefits will determine how much you can receive each month. If you are relatively young and are married, your monthly supplemental income will be low. This type of plan ideally is suited for a widow or widower who is at least 80 years of age. Younger retirees may want to establish a line of credit program that can be drawn upon as needed. Remember that principal and interest accumulate until the loan is repaid. Therefore, the amount of indebtedness can build up significantly when the loan is drawn upon.

16

SALE LEASEBACK PROGRAMS

Refinancing (Key 14) and reverse annuity mortgages (Key 15) involve taking on greater debt. If this bothers you, it still may be possible to cash out the equity in your home without moving. You may be able to arrange a sale contingent on your ability to rent the house back from the buyer. This is called a sale leaseback and is fairly common with commercial property. The idea of applying the concept to housing started in the San Francisco area but may be available in other parts of the country.

In a sale leaseback arrangement, an investor agrees to purchase the home, usually for something less than appraised value. The seller receives a sizable amount of cash from the buyer immediately as a down payment. The remainder of the price is financed usually on a ten- to fifteen-year mortgage, with the seller of the house providing the loan to the buyer. The mortgage provides a regular income stream for the seller. The buyer gives the seller a lease lasting as long as the seller wants to live in the home. The seller, in turn, pays rent to the buyer and the buyer is able to take advantage of tax benefits connected with owning rental real estate.

Here's an example. The home owner sells the home to the investor for $100,000. The buyer pays $20,000 at closing and gives a note for the $80,000 balance, payable monthly at ten percent interest over 15 years. This provides the seller about $860 per month in income. From this the seller pays $450 per month to the buyer as rent. The $20,000 down payment goes toward retiring an existing mortgage of $10,000, paying expenses of the sale and purchasing a deferred annuity to continue the income stream after the mortgage payments end. A *deferred annuity* is a series of periodic cash payments that begins sometime later, such as after ten years.

A sale leaseback can provide immediate cash, plus income for life and relieve the home owner of property taxes and other housing expenses (these are paid by the new owner). On the minus side, the retiree relinquishes equity and ownership rights in the home and any income tax benefits of home ownership. Fortunately, if he or she decides to move, the payments from the mortgage will continue until the end of the term. This income is for a strictly limited term, so the purchase of a deferred annuity is recommended highly. It also is good to place a limit on rent increases in the lease, because the income from the mortgage is fixed.

A major problem would occur if the investor defaults on the mortgage. This could occur if property values begin to decline in the area so that the investor's interest begins to look unprofitable. Some type of insurance might be arranged against this contingency.

Sale leasebacks should be structured carefully and documented. For information on programs and where they are available, contact the National Center for Home Equity Conversion, 110 E. Main St., Madison, Wisconsin 53703.

A similar transaction can be arranged by selling, or even donating, your home to a charitable organization with the stipulation that you can live in the home as long as you desire. This is called a *life estate agreement* or *charitable trust.* The price you receive for the home will be much lower than its market value. The difference between the home's market value and the sales price becomes a deductible donation that you can use to reduce your income taxes.

17

TRADING DOWN TO A SMALLER HOME

If you have decided to move, trading your present home for a smaller one can offer several advantages. First of all, you will be converting your equity to cash. Unlike refinancing, this is accomplished without taking on more debt. The proceeds of the sale are true income and won't have to be paid back in the future. Of course, a portion of the proceeds will have to be invested in a new home. However, if you buy a more modest home, you should have some cash left over to provide supplemental income for retirement.

Secondly, a smaller home should reduce your living costs. Expenditures for property taxes, insurance, and upkeep will be lower. You may find that the responsibilities for maintaining the household also are reduced as you will have less space to care for. By selling and moving, you may choose to live in an area that has a lower cost of living than your present location. This may mean moving to the suburbs as opposed to the core city. Or it may mean moving to another part of the country. If you do this, you probably should move somewhere you reasonably are familiar with instead of committing yourself to a community sight unseen. Lower cost may be deceptive if it entails giving up public services or other opportunities you value.

An example shows the potential of trading down. A couple sell their $250,000 home upon retirement. They have an existing mortgage of $50,000. From the sales price they pay off the old mortgage and the expenses of the sale, leaving them with $180,000 in cash. They move to another town and buy a smaller home for $100,000 cash. A portion of the remaining $80,000 is used to pay for moving expenses and minor remodeling; the rest is invested in a mutual fund providing monthly supplemental income. In addition, they no longer pay their usual $450 on the mortgage each month. They do have to pay property taxes and insurance on the new home of about $100 a month.

Trading down works best when you live in an area with an active housing market. This allows you to get top dollar for your home. If you move to an area with a depressed market, you can get a bargain on the replacement home. When investment opportunities are good—when relatively safe investments provide high yields—you may want to rent a replacement home instead of buying. At any rate, you should find out how much you are likely to get for your home and how much you must spend on its replacement.

You may decide to invest a large portion of your proceeds by buying the replacement home for cash. This is faster, relieves you of mortgage payments, and may allow you to drive a better bargain when buying the home. If investment opportunities are especially good, you may want to take out a mortgage and use the cash for investing. Risky or speculative investments should be passed over.

If you have trouble selling your old home, you might consider offering seller financing. You can set up the financing to provide you with monthly income. The rate of interest may be higher than you could get in alternative investments. Be careful to have the loan set up properly from a legal standpoint, and you may want to get a lending institution to underwrite the loan. Be leery of a buyer who does not want to pay a reasonable down payment. The more the buyer invests in cash, the less likely he or she is to stop making loan payments.

18

BUYING A CONDOMINIUM OR COOPERATIVE UNIT

When trading down to a small home, you may want to consider buying a unit in a condominium complex (*condo*) or cooperative building (*co-op*). These units usually are among the smaller and least expensive homes on the market (although some condos and co-ops are the most expensive homes when located in highly valuable areas, such as midtown Manhattan). Although often not appropriate for large families, they tend to be the ideal size for singles or childless couples.

Many complexes offer recreational amenities such as tennis courts and swimming pools. They often are located in urban areas close to shopping and medical services and along public transportation routes. They provide a measure of security and social interaction because of the close proximity of neighboring residents. Finally, many of the routine household chores, such as lawn maintenance, are taken care of by the management of the complex.

Owning a condo or co-op is significantly different compared with owning a detached home, and a prospective buyer should understand what he or she is getting into. When you own a condo unit, you have undivided ownership of the interior space within the confines of your unit. The other parts of the complex that you use are held in common ownership with the remaining unit owners. In practical terms, this means that a set of bylaws define what you are allowed to do with these common areas, including the exterior of your unit. By the same token, responsibility for upkeep and repair of these areas is shared among the owners.

When you buy a co-op, you actually are buying stock in a special corporation that owns the apartment building. As a shareholder, you are entitled to occupy a specified unit in the building, subject to a lease that runs indefinitely, that is, for as long as you remain an owner in good standing. As in a condominium, you are restricted in your use of the common areas in the building and are responsible for making repairs to your unit.

The proximity of neighbors and the fact that they share ownership of common areas make it important for residents to be compatible in lifestyle and attitude toward property improvements. Resident conflict is one of the worst things about living in condos and co-ops. Co-ops often carefully screen prospective buyers to make sure they will not cause problems fitting in with the other residents.

Condo ownership means membership in the owners' association, whereas co-op owners are shareholders in the corporation. Both organizations have governing boards composed of individuals elected by the body of owners to serve limited terms. These boards interpret and enforce the bylaws and make sure all maintenance and repair work is done.

All condo and co-op owners pay a monthly fee to provide the funds for maintaining the property. The fee may be called *rent* or *maintenance* in a co-op.

If you seriously are considering a condo or co-op, you may be interested in another book in Barron's Keys series, *Keys to Buying a Condo or Co-op*. It provides much more detail on these types of housing.

19

RENTING A HOME

There are three main reasons most people prefer to own their home rather than rent. First, they like the investment idea of housing. The money spent on the down payment and mortgage is thought to be invested rather than thrown away on rent. Second, they can save taxes by buying, because mortgage interest and property taxes are deductible if they itemize. Third, they can exercise control when they own. They can change the home to suit their desires and no landlord can raise their rent or refuse to renew the lease.

However, some of these advantages may not be very important when you are retired. Your taxable income may be low enough that the deductions for a home owner's expenses are worth little. This may be true especially if a large portion of your retirement income comes from Social Security. At most, only half of Social Security benefits are subject to tax. Each dollar of deductible expense may save only 15 cents in taxes. Remember that if you have no deductible expenses at all, you can use the standard deduction, which was made more generous by the 1986 Tax Reform Act.

Investment in a home is a long-term prospect, unless you are in a part of the country where housing prices are continuing to increase rapidly. Even in these areas, you don't know when the market will turn around leaving you with an overpriced asset. Housing investment is more risky today. Some markets have suffered big price drops and home owners are having trouble selling properties. An investment that takes many years to reach fruition may be of little value to a retiree.

On the other hand, renting has some real advantages. You can invest all of the proceeds from the sale of your old home in whatever asset you wish. You can use it to produce regular income and enjoy the liquidity of being able to get your money back when you need it. You don't have to worry about paying for repairs on a home or routine maintenance. If you don't like the place you are renting or want to move to another area, it is much easier to do when you are renting than when you own a home. Finally, there is a wide variety of rental housing in many areas. You can rent a small apartment, a townhouse, or a detached home.

The main disadvantage continues to be the loss of control when you live in someone else's property. You will be subject to periodic rental increases and your only defense is the right to move. You can try to lessen this problem by agreeing to a long-term lease with a provision for stable or gradually increasing rent. You will not be able to change the property as you please, although the landlord may be amenable to mutually acceptable improvements. When renting, it is preferable to find a place that suits you just as it is because you may not be allowed to make changes.

If tax deductions are not especially valuable in your situation, if you are not especially interested in building a property estate, or if attractive rental housing is available, you may consider the alternative of renting. There are even tax incentives to help you should you choose to rent (see Key 45).

20

MORTGAGE LOANS

If it has been a while since you've applied for a mortgage loan, you may find things quite different. You will find you have more options in the type of loan you can get. This suggests you must be more knowledgeable to get the right loan for your situation.

First, you will find more types of institutions who make mortgage loans. At one time, the local savings and loan association was your only source. Now, commercial banks commonly make house loans and mortgage banking companies are more prominent. To get a list of lenders, ask your real estate agent or look in the Yellow Pages under "mortgages." Try to get a recommendation from someone who has used a specific lender. You want a lender that will treat you fairly and process the loan promptly. Also, expect terms to vary significantly among lenders.

The fixed-rate loan is still the most popular form of mortgage loan. In addition, you may choose an adjustable-rate mortgage (ARM). The interest rate of an ARM may be changed at regular intervals, generally every year or every six months. The changes are governed by a special index. In general, when interest rates go up in the market, the rate on your ARM loan goes up. Likewise, an interest rate decline should cause your rate to drop. To insulate the borrower from unlimited increases in the rate (your loan payments go up each time the rate is increased), many ARMs have *caps,* limitations placed on the maximum change in the rate in any one period. These caps can be placed on the change during one year and on the total amount of change over the term of the loan.

If you live on a fixed income (or the income you receive does not rise with the inflation rate), you probably should avoid an ARM. Any substantial increase in your payments may cause you to cut your other expenditures severely or default on the mortgage. Default may mean losing your home. ARMs often are issued at much lower interest rates than fixed-rate loans. When the rate difference is large (about three percentage points or more), you might consider the ARM, particularly if it has caps. Even then, make sure your budget has enough leeway that you could handle higher loan payments. (If you would like to know more about ARMs and how to choose the best loan, see Barron's *Adjustable Rate Mortgages*.

Another choice available today is a fixed-rate mortgage with a a 15-year amortization (payoff) term. The monthly payments are a bit higher than a comparable 25- or 30-year mortgage, but you end up paying much less in interest over the life of the loan. If paying off your mortgage early appeals to you and you can afford the higher payments, you may consider a 15-year loan. These often carry a lower interest rate.

Many lenders make FHA-insured and VA-guaranteed mortgages. These are among the few loans available today that may be assumed by a subsequent buyer with no increase in the interest rate. A buyer may have to prove creditworthiness for the loan, but retention of the interest rate may appeal to you as a potential seller. In addition, there are mortgages insured by private companies that allow a five to ten percent down payment. These types of loans are primarily for first-time home buyers who don't have much cash to invest.

21

CO-BUYING WITH A FRIEND

Suppose you wish to move and buy a new home but don't need a great deal of space. You don't particularly like the formal structure of a condominium or co-op nor moving into a complex with a group of strangers. Possibly you are widowed or single and desire some form of companionship. You find that there are several attractive homes on the market in desirable locations but all are too large for your personal needs.

You may know someone in a similar situation. If you think you could get along reasonably well with this person, you might want to consider buying a home jointly. The two of you would pool your resources to purchase an appropriate home. If you need financing, both you and your friend can co-sign a mortgage loan document. This is relatively common (in some cases, young home buyers get their parents to co-sign a mortgage to ensure getting the loan) and no special type of mortgage instrument is needed. Also, most zoning and housing codes do not restrict such an arrangement, unless a large group plans to occupy a single-family home. There may be restrictions if only one party actually buys the home and rents out part of the house to the other. In that case, the arrangement might be construed as a boarding house or apartment house. If both parties are owners, there should be no legal problem.

Of course, many unforeseen things can happen when people share a home, especially if both have some type of ownership rights. It is recommended highly that some type of written agreement be drawn up that details specific responses to any contingency.

The agreement should cover the following as a minimum:

- How the house is to be divided physically. You may want to assign certain rooms to each party as private space with the rest of the home as common space. This will reduce arguments about how space is used.
- How responsibilities are divided. This includes sharing of household duties, financial responsibilities (such as paying mortgage payments, which will help in claiming tax deductions as well), and handling emergencies that may come up. You may find it acceptable to divide these responsibilities evenly, but put it down in writing so there will be no misunderstandings.
- Visits. Who can visit and where will they stay? What concessions should one party have to make for the other's visitors?
- Repairs and improvements. How should these be decided and how shall the costs be divided?
- Termination. This is one of the most important things to work out and one that you are likely to overlook when the arrangement is set up. If one party is unable to carry on his or her financial responsibilities, the other may have to step in and make up the difference. The consequences should be determined beforehand. Suppose one party dies or has to leave for some reason. Steps should be detailed for transferring that person's interest to the remaining party so that person is not forced to move, and for releasing the departing person from the mortgage obligation. For example, each party may set aside some money to buy out the other's equity. Life insurance can be used with each naming the other party to receive proceeds and buy

the other party's interest. That way family heirs will get cash without the need to sell the unit on their own. Finally, conditions need to be spelled out for deciding when and how to sell the property when the time comes. This should cover making the decision, how the property is to be sold and how the proceeds are divided. There also should be some documentation of funds that were supplied by each party when the property was purchased, especially if the burden was not divided equally.

22

RESORT LIVING

It used to be that retiring to the luxury of a resort was possible only for the very rich. Today, if you are careful how you select the place you go, you may be able to enjoy resort living on a relatively modest budget. Of course, we're not talking about Palm Springs or the French Riviera. Here are some possibilities:

- Convert your existing vacation home into a full-time residence. In this case, the property is something you already own. You will have to give up any rental income the property produced and can't claim depreciation on your income taxes, but you also will be giving up the expense of maintaining two homes. Before converting, make sure you can tolerate living in the area on a year-round basis. If you own a time share vacation home, this type of conversion is not feasible, because you would have to buy out other owners' interests.
- Buy into a retirement community with resort amenities. Many developments targeted to retirees have facilities specially attractive to older people. These include tennis courts, golf courses and swimming pools. Golf course developments often allow you to own a unit directly adjacent to the course. In addition, there are programs specially developed for residents.
- Buy a home in a town with resort qualities. Florida, Texas, Arizona, and Southern California are popular with retirees thanks to the favorable climates. Check out housing costs in the more attractive tourist towns or fishing villages in these areas. If you avoid the more

famous spots, you may find some very affordable homes in beautiful locations.

- Buy a home outside the United States. The cost of living may be much lower in areas like Spain, Mexico, Puerto Rico, and the Virgin Islands. You will be able to buy more home with less and all other expenses may be lowered as well. Income may be unchanged—Social Security pays the same amount no matter where you live.

However, there are drawbacks. You become subject to the political instability of the locale and may feel uncomfortable with or resented by the local populations. Banking and government services, such as police and fire protection may be inadequate. Medical services, public or private, may be far inferior to that in the United States. Finally, travel to see relatives may be expensive or difficult.

23

RETIREMENT COMMUNITIES

In the past ten years, developments aimed exclusively at independent, active retirees have become popular, particularly in warm weather retirement areas, such as Florida and Arizona. In general, these developments are large-scale, residential planned communities specially designed for one- and two-person households, with an emphasis on amenities and security. Residents usually are restricted to a specified age limit. The concept is that senior citizens prefer to live with people who share their lifestyles and want to be separated from young adults and children. If this idea appeals to you, you could consider living in one of these developments.

Retirement communities are a refuge from the larger world. Generally, there is some type of security system to limit who can enter the community. Residents and their guests are issued passes to enter security gates. Housing units are designed to aid in mobility. Multistory units are not uncommon, though often serviced with elevators. Recreational amenities include pools, tennis, and golf facilities. Open space and gardens are integrated into the plan to provide pleasant surroundings throughout the complex.

In addition to the recreational facilities, there often are planned social events for residents. This helps residents in becoming more active and familiar with their neighbors. There may be some type of emergency medical services on site. At a minimum, individual units are equipped with emergency communication devices for access to local ambulance service.

In general, retirement communities are targeted to the more active and affluent retirees. Most require purchase of units under a condominium-type arrangement. However, there are some rental projects and it may be possible to lease a unit in a condominium project. Plan on purchase prices and rental rates to be somewhat above those for comparable units outside the development.

Three major considerations in choosing this alternative are:

Affordability. Can you afford to live in the community? It may be that the higher living costs within the development require you to limit other expenses that add to your comfort. Check on the availability of financing. There may be special loans available that make a purchase more affordable.

Lifestyle. Do you like the idea of being surrounded by people your age or do you prefer a mix of ages? Some retirees may find a community a little too planned and structured and are bored being with "old people" all the time. As with any other alternative, how the housing fits into your preferred lifestyle and value system is one of the most important considerations.

Resale. Can you sell your unit, and what restrictions apply? If there is an age limit on residents, you face a restricted market if you want to sell. The management of the development may assist you in selling or may even purchase the unit back from you or your estate. If you are not sure this will be your permanent address, the ability to resell is important.

24

MOBILE HOMES

What used to be called a mobile home, today more accurately referred to as "manufactured housing," is one of the most inexpensive housing options. As a permanent housing choice, mobile homes have several disadvantages. First, unless you own the land upon which the home is located, you are subject to uncontrolled lease payment increases and losing your lease. Sites for mobile homes often are limited by local ordinances and may be banished to undesirable areas of town (some towns allow so-called "granny cottages," a housing unit placed on the same lot as an existing home, if the residents are related). The structure tends to be much more vulnerable to violent storms than site-built homes, which makes them somewhat dangerous, particularly if the resident is not in a position to evacuate quickly.

For most retirees, a traditional mobile home is not a desirable choice. A significant number of retirees are attracted to homes that truly are mobile—a motor home or trailer that allows them to live in different areas of the country over time. These usually are called *recreational vehicles* (RVs). A typical pattern is for a retired person or couple who have a home in the northern part of the country to spend the winter months living in a mobile unit in a warm climate. There are mobile home developments that cater specifically to this trade (such as "Sun City" in Arizona). These "snow birds" are able to enjoy a mild climate all year-round at a cost lower than maintaining two homes. The mobile nature of the home allows side trips along the way during the transition and side excursions during the winter stay.

When evaluating the cost of mobile living, consider that you will have the cost of maintaining your regular home for the full year (it may be possible to lease it out during the winter, if the idea appeals to you). You will need a home designed for moving, not one designed to be transported to a site and permanently attached. The more elaborate features and space you want, the more the unit will cost. Remember, however, that you will be spending a significant amount of time living in the unit, so don't cut too many corners on space and quality. Depending on the state in which the unit is licensed, you may have to pay personal property taxes on the vehicle. Finally, there will be rental charges and other fees at the site you choose to park the unit.

You can park the unit at a regular mobile-home park. But you may not be able to get a short-term lease and you may not find many neighbors who share your lifestyle. Alternatively, you could use a national or state park. The problem here is that you probably will be limited to a stay of a week or so. More than likely, you will be best off finding a park that caters to the seasonal commuter or is designed specially for retired people. In choosing a park, factor in the following information:

- What facilities are provided, how crowded are they, and are there special fees for their use?
- What utilities are available and what is the cost?
- What is the rental charge? Are there special long-term rates?
- How big are the sites? Is the design attractive and is there open space available?
- Is there storage space available for things you use infrequently, such as golf clubs, carts, or boats?
- How helpful, efficient, and reliable is the management? (If you have not stayed at the park, try to get recommendations from others who have.)

25

APARTMENT CONVERSION

Suppose you have decided not to move, yet you have too much space to keep up and could use some additional income. The ideal solution would be renting some of your excess space. A low-cost, flexible way to do this is to take in a boarder through a house sharing plan (see Key 13). Another alternative that provides more privacy for both tenant and owner is to convert part of your home into an accessory apartment.

An accessory apartment is a separate dwelling unit, complete with bath and perhaps a kitchen, built into a single-family home. Often, the unit is produced by converting a basement, attic, or garage. In addition, the tenant may have the use of other parts of the home, such as a den or living room.

The apartment may be a way for a retiree to avoiding moving by obtaining the financial assistance necessary to keep the house. The arrangement also can be psychologically supportive by giving the home owner a new responsibility and social contact. This may be valuable particularly for someone who has lost a spouse. To the extent that the home owner remains in the home, rather than moving or becoming institutionalized, the character of the neighborhood is maintained, yet additional housing is opened up for someone of limited means.

However, there are serious problems with the concept as well. The process of conversion may be costly. Expending funds up front with only the prospect of a paying tenant may discourage many home owners from the idea. Beyond the cost, such conversion may run afoul of local ordinances in many communities. Some localities have special zoning classifications for elderly accessory apartment units. Otherwise, conversion may not be possible. Another problem is getting good tenants. Most older home owners might be reluctant to take in a stranger and will need assistance in locating the appropriate tenant. Some areas have special programs to find tenants for accessory apartment providers. Check with your local agency in charge of housing or aging for any special programs in your area. A list of state agencies is printed at the end of this book (see page 139). Also helpful is the book, *Creating an Accessory Apartment,* by Patrick H. Hare and Jolene N. Ostler. The book, published by McGraw-Hill, offers a sample lease and other guides.

26

SUBSIDIZED HOUSING

Living in a housing project is an alternative that few look forward to but, nevertheless, provides a home to a significant number of elderly—mostly younger, single retirees. This is housing for those who have lost their home because they could not afford to keep it (either were evicted because of lack of rent money or had to sell because of high mortgage payments). Although subsidized elderly housing is basic, there are more people requesting placement than there are units available.

Subsidized housing for the elderly is developed by non-profit sponsors—generally religious or civic organizations—with special assistance from the federal government. The sponsor undertakes the building process and operation of the building. The government, through the 202 program of the Department of Housing and Urban Development (HUD), provides low-cost development loans and subsidizes the rent paid by tenants. The character of the projects runs the gamut from presentable, comfortable apartment buildings to poorly constructed public housing complexes with few tenant amenities. If this alternative is an option for you, arrange to visit available buildings before committing yourself.

To be eligible for 202 housing, a person must have income not higher than 50 percent of the median income for the locality. Your local housing agency or the local office of HUD can supply you with the appropriate income limits for your area. Most applicants are placed on a waiting list until a unit becomes available. You will need to maintain some alternative housing arrangement until your name comes up on the list. If you are selected, you will pay some rent. However, the rent paid is no more than 30 percent of your income. For example, if you receive income of $600 per month, the most rent you can pay is $180 per month.

Some complexes have dining areas and lounges. Older units may even have private balconies. A trend is toward smaller complexes (fewer units) with more limited features. The government is trying to phase out this type of specialized housing in favor of direct rent supplements to the needy living in regular housing available in the marketplace. The attractiveness of a complex will depend on how generous the sponsoring organization is in its provisions.

27

RETIREMENT COMMUNITIES AND FAIR HOUSING LAWS

Condominium developments and apartment complexes that cater to elderly households often advertise their policy of restricting residence to adults. This is a main selling point because older childless couples generally do not want the noise and confusion caused by young children. The problem is that these policies may come into conflict with federal Fair Housing Laws and, therefore, may not be enforceable.

The Fair Housing Law attempts to ensure that people are not discriminated against because of race, sex, or ethnic background when attempting to rent or buy a home. Recently, the law has been altered to include families with children. Families with children, particularly single mothers, often have difficulty finding a place to live because of restrictions against children. Thus, the new law is expected to improve the opportunities of families to find housing.

The change in the law was not intended to outlaw retirement communities. In fact, the change is aimed primarily at rental housing. However, a condominium is exempt from the law only if it can pass a three-way test. First, at least 80 percent of the units in the complex must be occupied by someone at least 55 years old. Second, the complex should offer facilities or services specially designed for the elderly. Third, the age restriction must be a specific policy of the complex, as embodied in the official documents of the condominium or co-op. For exemption, the complex must comply with all three requirements.

If maintenance of the sanctity of the retirement community is important to you (in other words, you would not want to see the complex opened up to families with children), there are a few things you can check. First, if the complex is primarily rental housing, there may be no way to retain the age restriction. If the complex is not located close to a school and units are not well suited to families, there will be little attraction for families, so entry by households with children probably will be limited severely.

Second, if your owner's association requests a survey of owners by age, you should cooperate to provide a complete count. The association is trying to gather evidence to gain exemption from the Fair Housing Law. Should a change in the bylaws of the condominium be needed to add to the evidence, you may help by voting for the necessary change. Some owners resist the change for fear that age restriction would limit the resale market of their unit. However, if the units are not suited for families, expressing the policy in the documents would have little effect on value, and effective enforcement may make the units more attractive to elderly buyers.

28

IN-HOME SERVICES

Just because your spouse or your retired parent requires some assistance to conduct the daily routine does not mean moving to some type of institutional environment. You may be able to stay home and receive the level of care you need and can afford. There may be several advantages:

- You avoid the trauma and disruption of moving, as well as the expense of buying and selling property. If the home is not too ill-suited to retired life and the location is acceptable, staying put may be best.
- You can tailor the amount of assistance to your particular needs. Many services come from separate providers. You can contract for any mix that you want, rather than accepting a comprehensive program provided at an elderly care or nursing home. Of course, if you need a wide variety of services, a comprehensive program probably will be more economical.
- You can supplement professional care with assistance from relatives, friends, and volunteers. Assisting a parent with all of his or her needs can be too demanding for those who have other job and family responsibilities. But periodic checks may do a lot of good toward reassuring the parent as well as cutting down on expenses.

The retiree retains some control over his or her life. By remaining in a private, familiar environment, you can surround yourself with the things you enjoy and maintain a protective distance from others. At the same time, you can welcome those who are providing needed assistance as well as visitors. If you are prone to being reclusive, however, this may work to reinforce those tendencies. An older person living at home needs occasional visits to guard against loneliness and isolation.

If you are staying home and do require some assistance, the first thing you may want to consider is some level of remodeling to make routine tasks easier (see Key 30). This can get expensive, but even minor changes can help.

Many older people find it difficult to keep up with the routines of housekeeping. Relatives can do small chores, accompany the retiree on shopping trips, or even pick up things at the store. You may want to subscribe to some type of meal service. In many towns, Meals on Wheels, a private, nonprofit program, delivers meals to the elderly with limited incomes. If you can afford it, there are professional home care companies that can provide regular cleaning and maintenance.

It also is possible to receive a level of medical care at home. Specialized services are available to help administer medication, bathe, change bandages, and provide minor medical checkups. The costs depend on how much medical expertise is required. The more routine tasks can be provided by unlicensed staff. The most expensive is care provided by a physician.

It is even possible, albeit expensive, to hire a manager who is trained specially to manage a comprehensive elderly assistance program. In contracting this level of service, or any type of home care service, check references, get recommendations if possible and seek advice from your local senior citizen agency. This will help protect you against fraudulent activities on the part of service providers.

29

MOVING IN WITH RELATIVES

Even though extended families rarely live together in the same town anymore, it is relatively common for parents who need care to move in with their children. Perhaps this is because both parties see the move as a short-term expediency. The trauma of the move is cushioned by the familiarity of the people the parent will be living with. For the children, taking in a parent may be less troublesome than finding an affordable accommodation somewhere else. In addition, you don't have to worry about the type of treatment that a parent will receive.

On the other hand, moving in with your son or daughter's family may mean a great loss of independence and even some amount of humiliation. You may have to subordinate your daily life to the established routine of their family. Recognize that making a place for you in their home causes some disruption of their lives, even though they are happy to have you with them. The arrangement can work if both sides realize that much accommodation is necessary and appreciate the willingness of the other party to compromise. If resentment crops into the relationship, neither party will be well served. In other words, the move should not be looked upon as merely a way to cut the costs of elderly care.

Under the best conditions, living with your children can recreate the multi-generational households typical of earlier times. Older members of the family were valued for their store of wisdom and experience. They enriched the family as the keepers of tradition and customs and dispensers of helpful advice.

Before deciding to consolidate households, consider the relationship you have with your parent or child. Would everyday contact strengthen the bonds developed when they were growing up? Or would old conflicts resurface and lead to constant bickering? There are worse things than living in an impersonal nursing home and one of them is staying with relatives with whom you don't get along.

Here are other things to consider:

- Are the accommodations adequate? Will moving in mean crowding for each member of the household? Is the house appropriate for you, considering your physical condition and mobility? Does living there severely compromise your privacy?
- If possible, seek some active role in the family's routine, such as watching the grandchildren or sewing. Being a contributing member will improve your self-esteem and reduce any disruption for the family.
- Consider how often your children move. If your son or daughter is relocated frequently, you face the possibility of traveling along with them or trying to find another home when they do move.
- How long would you have to spend alone? Do both household heads work full time during the day? If you need to be helped during the day, there may be an adult day care center (Key 32) or senior citizen center (Key 31) in the area where you can spend the day. You should also consider what happens when the family goes on vacation. If you don't want to or can't go along, you may be able to check into a nursing home on a temporary basis or have someone come to the house to care for you. However, these services are expensive.

30

REMODELING FOR MEDICAL REASONS

When suffering some type of disability, people often find great difficulty performing routine tasks. Some of these must be performed by others. But, with some modifications to the home, many could be accomplished satisfactorily either independently or with minor assistance. Nursing homes and hospitals are designed specially to accommodate people with disabilities. If you are staying home or living with relatives, you may be able to redesign your surroundings to achieve the same end.

One of the reasons to avoid going to an institution is the comfort of living in familiar surroundings. When remodeling, you don't want to recreate an institutional setting. You merely want to reduce the obstacles to your mobility. The remodeling should not be too severe. Concentrate on the following:

- Eliminate unnecessary obstacles and hazards. Climbing of stairs should be eliminated if possible. This can be done by arranging all necessary functions on the same floor, providing ramps on outside entrances, or even installing an elevator if needed.
- Provide handrails and other aids. These are helpful particularly in baths. Remote controlled televisions and lights might be helpful and require only minor investment.
- Facilitate medical care. A hospital type bed may help someone who must spend time bedridden. Accommodations for a visiting nurse or a place for medications and equipment are good additions. A plan

should be prepared to allow access by medical personnel and emergency evacuation in case you have to be taken to the hospital.

Consult your physician or a physical therapist before modifying your home. Determine the things that need to be done, then think about convenience features if funds are left over. Find out what modifications would be covered by any insurance policies you have. Hire reputable building contractors to perform the work. You may be able to remain in your home even though you need some medical attention.

31

SENIOR CITIZEN CENTERS

If you are living in your own home or with relatives and need some level of assistance, there are several options. Which one is most appropriate depends on how much assistance you require, particularly with regard to medical care.

First, if you have a major disability that requires constant care or have great difficulty with ordinary routine tasks, you probably should be in a nursing home (Key 36) or continuing care community (Key 33). An adult day care center (Key 32) can provide a good supplement to your normal accommodations. One can be helpful especially if you are cared for in your children's home, but must spend some time unattended while family members fulfill other responsibilities. Finally, if you don't need medical care on a continuous or standby basis, but would like some focus for your everyday experience, you might attend a senior citizen center.

These centers often are provided by nonprofit organizations or local governments as a place for older citizens to spend time during the day. They generally are provided free of charge except for occasional events that may require a moderate fee. The main thing they offer is supervision by nonmedical staff (though they may be trained as elderly social workers) and the companionship of other senior citizens. Retirees may gather for informal games or engage in planned social and recreational activities. To find out if such a center is available in your town, contact your local department on aging

32

ADULT DAY CARE CENTERS

Senior citizen centers can provide a good outlet for retirees who otherwise would spend much of their day alone. However, they offer no assistance for those requiring medical care. An adult day care center can provide such support and is a good supplement to home care for an elderly parent who suffers a minor disability. Center staff are trained specially to work with people with physical and mental limitations. In addition, the center should have medical personnel on hand and provisions for emergency care.

A good center offers activities designed to maintain physical dexterity and mental alertness. Meals are provided that are nutritious and tailored to individual dietary requirements. Occasional special events and excursions may be planned.

Expect day care services to cost from $20 to $40 per day, more if extensive personal attention is needed. Some centers are equipped to handle severely incapacitated patients, including those suffering from Alzheimer's disease. Fees may be tiered so that specific services are priced separately. In general, you may acquire services on a day-to-day basis, rather than having to commit to a long-term contract.

To find local centers, ask for recommendations from your local aging agency (see directory, page 139) or institutions that work with the elderly, such as geriatric hospitals and nursing homes. You may even hire a special consultant to find the best services available. For the name of a competent specialist, write to National

Association of Private Geriatric Care Managers, Box 6920, Yorkville Station, New York, New York 10128. You may want to screen centers on your list before actually using them. Try to find out the following:

- How pleasant is the atmosphere at the center? Too institutional? Too informal?
- What kind of activities are available? Are attendees well supervised or left to pass time on their own?
- What level of medical care is offered? Is there licensed medical staff and part time physician care?
- What is included in the fee?
- Is transportation provided? Many centers provide transportation to and from the center.
- How well is the center prepared for emergencies? Can an attendee easily be transported to a hospital if needed?

Centers are licensed or awarded certificates from state authorities in many areas. Although such approval is not a prerequisite, it does provide you with some assurance of a minimum level of service and quality.

33

CONTINUING AND LIFE-CARE COMMUNITIES

For retirees who basically are independent but need some type of occasional or standby care, a continuous care retirement community may be a good choice. Such facilities offer an intermediate ground between living on one's own and a full care nursing home. These communities provide private living units with auxiliary services, such as meals, maid service, and health care (as well as devices for emergency assistance within the living units). In addition, residents are surrounded by others the same age and similar medical condition.

Many of these communities require an entrance fee that provides a guarantee of lifetime occupancy and care. In addition, a monthly rent or fee is assessed to pay for the services. Although the entrance fee is about what you might pay for a home, you actually do not own your living unit, even though you may have an unlimited right to stay in the unit for as long as you want and are able. If it becomes apparent that you need more intensive care, you may be transferred to a nursing home, often on the same site. Other communities, which technically are not true continuing care communities, operate on a strict rental basis with no entrance fee. In these homes, there is no guarantee of future medical care, although residents can acquire care for additional fees.

Communities are operated by profit-seeking and non-profit organizations. Some are provided by government agencies with fees based on residents' ability to pay. The quality of the buildings and grounds, as well as the medical services provided, vary greatly and tend to correspond to the entrance fee and rent charged. In general, there are three levels of care within the field of continuing care retirement communities:

Unlimited care. Also called *life-care,* these communities guarantee a full level of care for the resident's lifetime. Full services are provided, including three meals a day. Entrance fees are relatively high ($50,000 to $150,000) and monthly fees average around $1,000. Fees vary depending on the part of the country where the community is located.

Limited care. A basic level of medical care is provided for the entrance fee with extra care available for an additional fee. Usually only one meal is included. Entrance fees run $30,000 to $100,000 with monthly fees around $700. This may be a good choice for younger retirees who currently require little assistance. Full care communities may charge higher fees for younger residents because the potential cost of future care is higher.

Pay as you go. These communities provide a living unit with meals and medical care available on a "menu" basis. You pay for what you use with no guarantees provided of future service. Entrance fees are relatively low ($20,000 to $50,000) and so are monthly fees ($500).

Some inadequately financed communities have had financial problems and have even gone bankrupt. In such a case, residents may lose their investments and be left without the home and care they thought they had purchased. Unfortunately, financial data is hard to obtain, but you should try to get a financial statement when shopping. Perhaps your CPA can help. Also, look for a community that appears to have high occupancy, as vacancies are one sign of impending problems. The Continuing Care Accreditation Commission (1129 20th St., N.W., Suite 400, Washington, D.C. 20036) maintains an accreditation system and can send you a list of approved communities. Although not foolproof, knowing that the community has been inspected and approved may give you some peace of mind.

If possible, devote some time to making your choice and plan far enough ahead so that you don't have to make a last minute decision. Look carefully at the quality of the community and where it is located. Base much of your decision on how comfortable you will be living in the community. You will need to decide on the level of care you want, and how much assurance you desire of future care. Of course, this will have to be tempered by the resources you can afford to devote to the entrance and monthly fees. In some cases, entrance fees are refundable in full or part after you move in. However, expect refundable fees to be higher than nonrefundable fees.

If your resources are limited and you are not concerned about leaving an estate, you may opt for the nonrefundable fee option. Also inquire about entrance requirements. In many cases you must pass a physical exam. This is to screen out those with severe medical problems who cannot be accommodated by the community. You may be required to carry certain types of insurance, such as Medicare supplement policies or long-term care insurance. Because these policies are expensive if purchased late in life, determine if you must incur the extra expenses

34

FOSTER CARE

Even though certain individuals need constant attention or special medical care, they may not have to be institutionalized. They may be able to stay in the comfortable and reassuring surroundings of home and bring in the professional assistance they need. The cost of these services is high, with most provided on a per hour basis. General cleaning and nonmedical assistance runs about $5 to $8 per hour, whereas a registered nurse could cost $30 to $50 per hour. Some of these costs are covered by insurance or Medicare.

To obtain a program of services suitable for you, you may want to see a professional geriatric counselor. For a fee, the counselor can set a program and refer you to the best providers. Ask your local aging agency for a list of counselors. You may also consider remodeling to make your home more convenient and improve mobility (see Key 30).

It may be unreasonable from a financial standpoint to hire all the assistance you need. When medical disabilities are major, staying at home may become an unaffordable luxury, though the availability of in-home care may postpone the day when you must move.

There are some adult foster homes that provide a family setting, as contrasted with an institutional atmosphere. These are limited to a few residents, so each might have a waiting list. Check on license requirements of these places.

35

CARING FOR A DEPENDENT PARENT

A program of professional care for a medically dependent person living at home can be expensive (see Key 34) and probably is beyond most retirement budgets. The cost can be reduced significantly, however, if you can accommodate such patients in your home or monitor their condition in their home. This eliminates the need for a nonmedical professional to watch the patients and assist them with routine functions.

Although you may be able to provide all necessary assistance to someone who is semi-independent, for a totally dependent person you will need help from both medical and nonmedical professions. There will be a need for periodic examinations by physicians and possibly special cleaning or other procedures that should be performed by medically trained personnel. In addition, there may be times of the day when you are not available. As a supplement, you may consider adult day care (Key 32), if the center is prepared to accept patients with more serious disabilities (some can even handle patients with Alzheimer's disease).

When evaluating the decision to care for your dependent parent, rather than sending him or her to a nursing home, consider the following:

- Even highly dependent people need company. To the extent possible, try to assimilate them into your family life, rather than relegating them to an isolated room. In addition, they may desire contact with others of their own age. This is one advantage of using day care facilities, if available. At the center, they can interact with others in a monitored and controlled environment.

- Caring for a disabled spouse or parent can be a demanding job. You may find you need a break from time to time. A change and release of responsibility will improve your outlook, relieve the strain on your family, and probably refresh the relationship. You probably will need to make provisions for a temporary residence at a nursing home or hospital. Try to choose a place that will make them feel they are taking a vacation as well; consider the provision of small amenities and pleasant surroundings, not too institutional.
- Make ample provision for responding to an emergency. Know how to get in touch with an ambulance service and physician. You may want to learn some emergency procedures, such as CPR, to buy time before the professionals arrive. Ask the physician for recommended first aid skills that are appropriate for your parent's condition.

With the appropriate mix of your attention and professional care, you may be able to provide a suitable home for a dependent spouse or parent. Ideally, the choice will not hinge entirely on financial factors. Taking in your disabled father or mother (or other relative) should be approached from the standpoint of what is best for them. However, if the arrangement is highly restrictive to your family and your parent, it probably will not be the best solution.

36

NURSING HOMES

The most intensive level of care available for the elderly is provided in nursing homes. Nursing homes are institutions in the sense that a high level of control is exercised over residents' lives to protect their health and security. In general, residents of nursing homes need this level of security because their ability to control their own lives is impaired by physical or mental deterioration.

Nursing homes are a last resort when you are caring for an aged parent and a home setting is not feasible or sufficient for the person's needs. Placing parents in a home does not mean that you are putting them away or abdicating your responsibility for their care. Indeed, choosing a quality home and helping them adjust to new surroundings are a major part of providing care for parents who must be institutionalized.

The level of care provided in a nursing home is not standardized. The intensiveness of care may vary from the most stringent to a relatively minimal level. The more intensive the care, the more the home resembles a hospital, with residents spending much of their time in beds and most staff wearing hospital-styled uniforms. This level of care is for those who can do very little unassisted and who are suffering from severe medical problems. Nursing homes of this type are referred to as *skilled care* homes.

At the less intensive end of the scale, the home looks less like a hospital and more like a residential hotel. There is more opportunity for residents to move about on their own and more organized activities. At this level, the distinction between a nursing home and a retirement home (Key 33) becomes blurred. In fact, homes of this type may be called *personal care homes,* or *board and care* or *custodial care,* rather than nursing homes.

In many cases, a home will provide various levels of care in different wings or buildings within the complex. Some continuing care retirement communities have nursing homes on site. This facilitates moving residents into more intensive care units when the need dictates.

The movement into a nursing home is a very significant decision. Although not pleasant to contemplate, the sooner the possibility is confronted and planned for, the easier will be the transition. Better homes will have waiting lists. If you are not on a list when it comes time to obtain the services of a nursing home, you may have to settle for a much less desirable home. Another advantage of planning ahead is the opportunity to involve the older person in the decision process. This will give him or her a better feeling about the move and allow more time to prepare for the change. This is one major advantage of moving to a full service retirement community. Often, as part of the entrance fee, the resident is guaranteed a place in the nursing home when needed.

Nursing homes are expensive, with annual costs running from $20,000 to $50,000. Generally, Medicare and private insurance plans do not contribute fully to the cost until the resident's assets have been exhausted.

When inspecting homes, look for the following features:

- Efforts by the staff to maximize residents' activities. Areas should be designed to encourage activity and interaction among residents. If most residents appear to be passively waiting for time to go by, that may be a sign that little is being done to involve them.
- Broad visiting privileges for family members. Fre-

quent visits are important to condition both the resident and the family to the change. If visiting is severely restricted, it could indicate that the home does not want family members to see what the resident's daily life is like.

Of course, as the level of service required intensifies, there will be less activity afforded and less access to visitors. This makes it important that various levels of care be available and that the appropriate level be applied.

37

THE NURSING HOME PROBLEM

The move to a nursing home, whether for a short or long term, is a difficult one for the retiree and his or her family. Patients may feel that they are being deserted by their family, and left to suffer in an institutional environment. When faced with this situation, you will want to arrange the best match between the patient's needs and what the home has to offer. Your ability to do that may be highly compromised by the general shortage of good nursing homes in most areas.

Nursing homes are regulated in most states. Part of this regulation is to assure that a minimum level of care and safe procedure is provided. Another part of the regulation serves to restrict the number of homes operating. Every state, except Texas, Arizona, and Colorado requires approval before a new nursing home can be built. The core of the approval process is a certificate that indicates that a new facility is needed and is not a duplication of service. Such procedures often are used by regulatory agencies as a sort of reward to the industry for complying with service requirements. With entry to the market restricted, existing homes are protected from too much competition. Unfortunately, this has led to low vacancies (which means a lack of choice for consumers) and high costs. The occupancy rate for homes today is 96 percent.

Rising demand is making the problem worse. More people are living beyond the point they can care for themselves, putting pressure on medical care facilities. At the same time, changes in the Medicaid program encourages hospitals to discharge patients before they are fully recovered. This means more people require the services of a nursing home after hospitalization.

In July 1990, a Federal jury in Mississippi awarded damage verdicts to families of nursing home patients who had been neglected during their last years. Their nursing home was run by the largest national chain of nursing homes. Damages were awarded for the kind of routine neglect that occurs in homes, not for gross negligence. Abuses included leaving patients in their own excrement, verbal abuse by the staff, not bathing a patient, keeping a patient in a smelly room, and failing to give physical therapy that was needed. Whether these cases will have an effect on nursing home care or costs is too soon to determine.

Under these conditions, your choices may be limited severely. If you can afford to remain on a waiting list prior to entrance, you may have a better chance of getting what you want. Prior arrangements may be made, possibly through a retirement community, for future entrance when needed. Finally, if you are not relying on Medicaid to pay for the home, you may have more options. Many homes do not seek approval for Medicaid certification because of the red tape.

38

RETIREMENT PLANNING

Retirement, like other major events in your life, should be prepared for well ahead of time. This may be difficult if you are forced into early retirement because of loss of health or employment. Most people can judge when they will retire and should plan for the change. It is important that you line up your finances so that you will have a sufficient source of income and wealth to allow you to live the type of retirement existence you desire. In addition, you may need to start early to gain access to retirement homes or other accommodations.

Most people rely on several sources of income in retirement. If you have been employed, you are eligible for Social Security benefits and probably some type of pension benefits from your current or previous employers. Many people continue to work after retiring from full-time employment and, therefore, have wage or salary income. Others run businesses in retirement and obtain profits from those endeavors. Ideally, you will have some investments put away that provide additional income. These are the building blocks from which you can fashion the foundation of your retirement plans. Review Keys 1 and 2 for considerations on figuring how much you will need and evaluating what you have.

The following are things that you should consider when starting your retirement planning:

- When deciding to go into full retirement, consider how difficult it will be to replace the income from your job. Even if you have enough savings to replace your after-tax income, you will have to pay some taxes out of pocket rather than through paycheck deduction. Also, you may have to arrange your own health insurance plan and savings program. You may want to explore the possibility of working past retirement, both to supplement your income and to provide you with something to do. Working on a temporary basis can be a good transition to full retirement. Possibilities include contracting with your old employer on a part-time or consultant basis, operating your own business, or even trading services for goods on an informal basis.

- You may need to restructure your investments to meet the needs of retired life. Even though your emphasis will be income production, don't shortchange the need for principal growth. You may be spending only the interest, but inflation constantly is eating away at the principal. Consider some inflation hedging assets, if possible. This can include common stocks, especially those related to natural resources, such as oil or gold. Home ownership is an excellent hedge.
- Include in your plans contingencies for the possibility that you may be disabled or lose your job before the time you intend to retire. Also consider what might happen if you lose your spouse before, or early into, retirement.
- Consider purchasing an annuity. A *deferred annuity* will provide you income for life beginning at a specified time in the future or age. This is protection against outliving your assets. An *immediate annuity* begins a payout in the month after it is purchased. Annuities are sold by insurance companies.
- Don't rely too heavily on Social Security or even private pensions. Plan on supporting your desired re-

tirement lifestyle with investment income and work income. Your Social Security benefits then can be thought of as a useful supplement.

- If you are not saving at least ten percent of your income (include your contribution to a savings program or Individual Retirement Account), try to beef up your savings. The earlier you start, the more you will have to work with when the time comes to retire. Whereas it does not make sense to squirrel away all your money and live like a monk, too much emphasis on living for today may leave you in dire straits when your employment stops.

Try to form a good idea of how you want to spend your retirement. Most people continue to live much as they did when they worked, making adjustments only when their health or finances force them to. Others take the opportunity to change their lives—traveling or moving to a better climate. Often people find retirement a difficult transition and abandon activities they thought they would enjoy. If you can come to grips early on as to what you want to do, your planning can take more shape and you will have a more clear-cut goal. Just remember to be flexible so you don't get trapped.

39

MEDICARE AND OTHER SHORT-TERM ASSISTANCE

Medical expenses can be financial burdens at any age, but the chances of major medical bills increase dramatically as you get older. Insurance for major medical expenses provided through your employer protects you while you are working. Often, these policies do not continue after you retire, leaving you vulnerable to the major expenses of serious illness.

Fortunately there are several government and private programs that can help. None are intended to meet all the costs of care, but can help get the services you need without depleting your savings. The programs discussed here are not sufficient to cover chronic disability, such as permanent residence at a nursing home (see Key 40 for long-term care insurance). They are designed to assist you in meeting emergency or periodic medical needs.

Medicare A is provided without charge to anyone over the age of 65. The program helps pay for hospitalization, outpatient care and temporary residence at a nursing home offering skilled medical care. Benefits are limited. You pay a deductible. (You pay the full amount of costs up to a specified limit. These amounts vary over time, so check with a Medicare office or the hospital's financial office to determine the limits.) Medicare then pays a portion of eligible costs over a limited period of time. After that time, you pay all costs. You can receive Medicare benefits more than once, but there is a lifetime reserve of so many days of assistance. After the reserve is depleted, you can receive no more help.

For a nominal premium, you can purchase Medicare B coverage. The benefits are similar to Medicare A, except they significantly are more generous. The deductible is much lower and the proportion of costs reimbursed is higher. Medicare pays benefits based on "reasonable costs" as determined by their staff. Unless the hospital charges are within the guidelines, you must make up the difference.

Private insurance companies offer a policy intended to supplement Medicare benefits. This "medigap" insurance will pay deductibles and some of the costs imposed on the patient, but there still may be some costs left over that you must take care of.

When all benefits are used up and your personal resources have been exhausted, you may be eligible for Medicaid. This is a program provided by the federal government for older people with little or no resources in the face of medical expenses. To receive Medicaid assistance, you must have depleted your resources (you are allowed to own a home up to a limited value) in the course of obtaining medical care. You are not allowed to transfer assets to relatives to qualify.

In general, the major medical insurance benefits you receive when employed provide good to excellent protection. You may want to inquire as to whether you may extend coverage after retirement by paying an annual premium (expect it to be high as you get older). If not, find out if you are eligible as a consultant or part-time employee. If so, you may consider such an arrangement with the company.

40

LONG-TERM CARE INSURANCE

Medical insurance and Medicare do not cover the costs of long-term care following an illness, such as a lengthy stay in a nursing home. Yet these costs can be devastating, particularly if the disability is permanent or chronic. Recognizing the burden of the costs, Congress passed a Catastrophic Health Care program funded by a special tax on Social Security recipients. However, protests over the impact of the tax forced a repeal of the program shortly after its introduction.

In the 1980s, insurance firms began offering a policy that does cover these costs, recognizing the longer survival rates of the population and the increased demand for long-term care. Long-term care insurance pays a portion of the costs of nursing homes (Key 36), adult day care (Key 32) and even home care (Keys 28 and 34). Generally, any care not provided in a hospital as direct treatment for an illness is eligible.

The extent and scope of coverage varies with each policy. Typically, benefits consist of reimbursement of expenses up to a specified limit per day or per month, with a lifetime benefit limit. You may be able to buy higher or lower limits on benefits.

There usually is no age limit when you can receive benefits. Conditions existing at the time of buying the policy may not be covered or are subject to a delay before being covered. This is to prevent someone buying a policy to treat a condition that already exists. It is wise to purchase the policy at a relatively young age to cover the possibility of needing care in the future.

Like life insurance, premiums increase sharply as the age of the beneficiary increases. Generally, premiums are fixed at the time the policy is purchased (so are benefits). You can buy an individual policy or subscribe to a group policy if offered through your employer or other organization to which you belong.

Because long-term care is so expensive, so is the insurance. One way to reduce the cost is to limit the benefit to a certain period of time, such as 30 months. This reduces the cost of even high quality insurance programs. Yet 30 months may be sufficient to do the financial planning that may be needed. If one transfers assets to children within 30 months of Medicaid assistance, the transfer will be voided and the asset must be used up before Medicaid will pay (see Key 46). But the individual can give valuable assets to children just prior to entering a nursing home and use private insurance for 30 months. Then, Medicaid can be used without disturbing the transfers.

Do you need long-term care insurance? Consider that one of four elderly persons spends some time in a nursing home (the odds are one in three for women). A much smaller proportion will stay for more than a year (which might make the insurance highly valuable). Only eight percent of women and five percent of men require care for more than a year. If you are in normal health, your chances of using the benefits are relatively low. Also consider that even the best policy will not cover the entire expense. The limited benefits you purchase are fixed when you buy the policy and may be insignificant by the time they are needed.

If you are interested, you can get a free guide. Write for "The Consumer's Guide to Long-Term Care Insurance" from the Health Insurance Association of America, 1025 Connecticut Avenue, N.W., Washington, D.C., 20036

41

SOCIAL SECURITY

During the Great Depression of the 1930s, a great deal of social legislation was passed under the New Deal of President Franklin Roosevelt. The idea was to provide a safety net of government support so that people would not have to become totally destitute regardless of their financial foresight or bad fortune. One of the most prominent of these programs is Social Security, aimed at helping retired people who have worked for employers covered under the program.

Social Security payments can be used for any purpose you desire. Although Social Security is intended as an income supplement not be relied upon as a sole source of support for retirement, it can provide an important supplement to your pension benefits and income from savings. In addition, there are special benefits should you be forced into retirement due to a physical disability and survivor benefits for dependents of covered employees who die prior to retirement.

As part of your retirement planning, you should find out how much support to expect from the program. Your benefits are based on your average earnings for a specified number of years that you were employed in a job covered by Social Security (most employment other than federal civil service, the military, and some government employers who have opted out of the system). If you are still employed, you won't be able to get an accurate estimate, because your remaining years of employment will determine the benefit level. You can get an estimate of your benefits by writing to the

Social Security Administration, P.O. Box 57, Baltimore, Maryland 21203 or calling 1 (800) 234-5772.

You can start receiving benefits when you reach the age of 65. If you want to retire before that age, you can receive benefits starting at age 62 (60 if you are a widow or widower). Benefits will be reduced by 20 percent (the reduction is prorated for retirement between 62 and 65 years of age). Of course, early retirement also eliminates the last several years of earnings from the calculation. So if you are at your peak earnings, early retirement may penalize you in two ways: a reduction in benefits and reduced average earnings upon which benefits are based.

Until you are age 70, you are restricted in how much part-time earnings you can make. The limit increases each year according to inflation. In 1990, it was $9,360 for retirees over 65 and $6,840 for those under age 65. There is no limit for retirees over 70 years of age. Your benefits are reduced by one dollar for each three dollars (two dollars if under 65) you earn over the limit. The limit and reduction does not apply to money received from pensions or investments, only earnings from your own labor.

Spouses and children of eligible retirees also may be entitled to benefits, provided the marriage lasted more than a year. Eligible relatives include unmarried children under 18 (if severely disabled, benefits may extend past the age of 18), a spouse who is 62 or older (or any spouse caring for a child under 16 who is eligible for disability benefits), and, under some circumstances, grandchildren or great-grandchildren.

A worker, or dependents, may receive benefits before retirement age if he or she is disabled. Disability means you are impaired to the extent you can't work and the disability is expected to last at least one year or to be terminal. In addition, you need a smaller number of credits (based on your time in employment) to qualify for disability benefits. Disability benefits are reduced by any other disability income you receive from workman's compensation or other pension programs.

The retirement age with full (unreduced) Social Security benefits is being raised to age 67 (currently 65) with the increased age phased in gradually. People born before 1938 will not be affected.

The phase-in schedule is shown below:

Year of Birth	**Normal Retirement Age**
1937 or earlier	65
1938	65 and 2 months
1939	65 and 4 months
1940	65 and 6 months
1941	65 and 8 months
1942	65 and 10 months
1943-54	66
1955	66 and 2 months
1956	66 and 4 months
1957	66 and 6 months
1958	66 and 8 months
1959	66 and 10 months
1960 and later	67

42

STATE ASSISTANCE PROGRAMS

Almost every state has some form of assistance program aimed at helping older citizens gain appropriate housing. In general, these programs are for people of very limited resources. Some are valuable to any elderly person who needs help in cutting through the confusing array of options provided in today's market. Check with your state's agency on aging (see directory, page 139) for details and eligibility requirements.

Here is a sampling of some of the types of programs operating in various states:

Home Equity Conversion. (See Keys 15 and 16.) These programs help those with homes who desire additional income for retirement or need the income to keep their home. Programs range from regulations on who may offer reverse annuity mortgages and loan terms, to direct loans and sale leaseback programs from the state. Wisconsin and California have been leaders in the home equity conversion field, but other states have introduced programs as well.

Property Tax Breaks. (See Key 45.) Reduced property taxes for elderly home owners is a popular idea among state legislators. The objective is to help older home owners reduce the costs of home ownership and allow them to stay in their homes. The assistance usually takes the form of increased homestead exemptions on the assessed value of the home or refunds of taxes once they are paid. Check with your local tax assessor's office.

Home Sharing. (See Key 13.) Several states encourage and assist older home owners to share their homes with other older people. The most common type of assistance is a matching service that attempts to link willing home owners with others in the community that need housing. A program in North Dakota fosters home sharing between elderly home owners and college students, in which the students provide home maintenance services.

Accessory Apartments. (See Key 25.) The biggest problems encountered with providing an accessory apartment (converting a portion of a single-family home into an apartment that can be rented to an elderly or nonelderly tenant) are the costs of conversion and legal barriers to adding rental units within a single-family neighborhood. Some states help by providing special low cost loans for conversion and by overriding zoning restrictions. A few states operate Elderly Cottage Housing Opportunity (ECHO) housing programs in which home owners are allowed to provide temporary dwelling units for an older relative within their homes or on the same lot.

Congregate Housing. (See Key 33.) Several states encourage the production of subsidized retirement/care housing for those of limited income by providing low interest loans to sponsors. The loans allow development, conversion, or acquisition of appropriate structures. Other programs offer certification of continuing care retirement communities to help people choose the proper community for an older relative.

Day Care. (See Key 32.) Many communities operate senior citizen centers (Key 31) at nominal or no cost. Patients who need more skilled supervision require the services of adult day care centers that charge a substantial daily fee. States do offer assistance in paying these fees for those of limited resources. Such financial assistance may allow many families to house elderly parents within their own homes and avoid having to institutionalize older relatives who need medical care.

Counseling. With the proliferation of specialized services for the elderly, there often is a need for help in finding the right type of service and arranging financing. Several states provide counseling services for elderly citizens to present the options available and help them choose. Others publish directories of retirement communities, centers, and sources of assistance for older citizens.

43

REAL ESTATE AS AN INVESTMENT

Whether or not you own a home and plan to keep it in retirement, you may consider owning other real property for its investment income. Real estate has a reputation for providing high rates of return, maintaining value compared to inflation, and providing tax benefits. A drawback is that it may not be an ideal source of level income needed by a retiree.

Some of the disadvantages of real estate investment are onerous especially for a retired investor. When you acquire properties, you are competing with other investors who are looking to make a high return through appreciation. Therefore, the yield you receive from rent may be low compared to the price you must pay to get the property. Many real estate investors expect the property to produce negative cash flow (the excess of revenues over current expenses) for several years. If your main goal is to obtain current income, real estate may not work.

In essence, real estate should be perceived as a long-term investment. Buying and selling property is expensive and time consuming. If the market is not active when you need to sell, you may suffer a drastic reduction in value. Therefore, real property is not a good place to put funds that you may need in an emergency. On the other hand, you can refinance property to get cash for emergencies. A drawback of refinancing is that it is expensive and may not be practical when interest rates are high.

A third disadvantage is the supervision that real estate requires. The property must be maintained physically. Even if you hire a contractor to do the work, you may be hit with costly repairs when you need the money for other things. You also will need to attract and contract with tenants, as well as handle their problems when they complain. This is one reason for not owning property far from where you live (also, if the property is in another state, you may be subject to taxes from both states). You can get a manager to take care of these problems, but you have to find someone you trust to do the job effectively.

Regardless of these disadvantages, there are some situations where real estate can provide benefits to a retiree. A strategy of buying properties in your earlier years to provide income in later years is a good one. Ideally, you acquired properties when prices were attractive and they are more valuable in today's market. You may have retired most of the mortgage debt on the properties. You can now refinance to gain cash for your retirement or enjoy rental income with little outlay for debt service. By having a lot of equity, you are less vulnerable to periods of slack demand when rental income can fall. Even though you will not get much tax benefit from older property (depreciation has run out and your interest expense is low), this may not be important if you are in a low tax bracket. (See Key 45.)

Finally, some retirees who are looking for money-making activities during retirement may seek out a small apartment building or motel to own and manage. You may find this endeavor rewarding, especially if you desire to work with people and have the energy and mobility to maintain a property and a business. But be careful not to underestimate the time and work such ventures will require.

44

PENSIONS

Social Security never was intended to be the sole source of support for retirement. Therefore, the federal government has provided tax incentives to encourage people to invest part of their earnings in retirement plans. There are various ways you can participate in these plans, such as contributing into your employer's qualified pension plan, setting up your own Keogh plan (if self-employed), contributing to a tax-deferred annuity program, or starting an Individual Retirement Account (IRA). Depending on the program, you can take advantage of matching contributions from your employer, deferment of taxation on fund earnings, and possible deduction of contributions from taxable income.

When you retire and begin to withdraw funds from your pension accounts, you must pay taxes on the income received. This includes all employer contributions, account earnings, and any contribution you made from pre-tax income. There also are rules on how you can receive your benefits. Failure to comply can result in sizable penalties in addition to taxes due.

In most plans you can't take any of your money out before you are 59½ years old. On the other hand, you must begin to receive at least part of the money by April 1 of the year after you become 70½ years old. If you withdraw your account early, you face a fine of ten percent of your accumulation, plus income taxes become due. There may be no penalty if you receive benefits from an employer's plan when you leave the job. There also is no penalty if you receive benefits from a spouse's plan as part of a divorce settlement or if you need the money to pay medical expenses. As far as complying with the rules on minimum withdrawals, it is recommended you have a tax expert set up a schedule of payouts according to the law. Failure to take benefits in a timely fashion can result in very large penalties.

There are several ways you can make withdrawals after you reach retirement age. The method you use depends on your financial needs and your tax situation. You can set up an annuity that will provide periodic income over time. The money is taxed as it is received. If some of the payout represents contributions from income on which you already paid taxes, you will owe taxes on only a portion of the receipts. After you have received an amount equal to your contribution, all subsequent income is taxable.

Alternatively, you may receive the entire account in one lump sum payment. Obviously, if the whole amount were taxable, a lump sum distribution could push you into the highest tax rate. To avoid this situation, you are allowed to figure your tax by "averaging" the distribution. See your tax accountant for guidance on the best way to take distributions from your account.

45

TAX CONSIDERATIONS

Unfortunately, retirement doesn't end your obligations to pay income taxes. To the extent you earn income, own property or spend, you will continue to help pay the costs of government. There are some special situations you may take advantage of, and a few suggestions to consider are offered.

- Selling your home. If you have been a home owner for a number of years, you may have a substantial capital gain on paper. The tax laws allow you to defer paying taxes on gains as long as you buy a replacement home of at least the same value as the one you sold within two years of the sale. All taxes that were deferred from previous sales come due when you sell and do not replace the home with one of equal value.

When you retire, you may want to sell your home and use the proceeds to support your retirement. This means you will rent or buy a place that costs much less. The tax laws provide you with an escape.

If you (or your spouse) are over 55 years of age, and have used the home as a principal residence for three of the past five years, you may sell a home and exclude up to $125,000 of accumulated profits from taxation. This is a permanent exclusion, not a deferment. However, you can do this only once in a lifetime. If you hold the home jointly with your spouse, you are treated as a single person for purposes of the exclusion. That is, if either spouse meets the age, holding period, and use requirements, both spouses are treated as meeting them.

There are some interesting and useful wrinkles to the

requirements. The three year requirement for use and dwelling need not run simultaneously. That is, a taxpayer could qualify by having been a tenant for two years, then buy the house, live there for one more year, then vacate but own for two more years.

For sales after September 30, 1988, a taxpayer will meet the required use rule if he became physically or mentally incapable of self care during the five year period before the sale. Other requirements are that he owned and used the residence for at least one year of the five years preceding the sale, and any time during the five years he lived in a facility that is licensed to take care of individuals who are incapable of self-care.

- Homestead programs for the elderly. Many localities allow special exemptions from property taxes for home owners over 65. Sometimes special provisions, called circuit breakers, prevent tax from exceeding a certain amount. You have to apply for the exemption to get the benefits. This can save you tax dollars if you own a home. Check with your city, county, or school district tax office for information.
- Claiming a parent as a dependent. If you are supporting a parent by providing at least half of their living expenses (if you are taking care of your parent in your home, you probably qualify), you may claim an additional dependent on your income tax return. You may be considered a head of a household and use the more favorable tax rate chart, whether your parent is in your house or in a care-providing institution. Also, you may be able to deduct medical expenses that you pay for your parent, though they must exceed 7.5 percent of your adjusted gross income to receive any benefit.
- Check your marginal tax rate. Most people's taxable income decreases when they retire. If your income is lower, your marginal tax rate may be lower as well.

This means that the way you invest now may be different than when you were working. Buying a municipal bond or other tax-exempt investment may not be worthwhile when your tax rate drops. Owning a home may no longer be beneficial from a tax standpoint. Your marginal tax rate is the amount of each additional dollar that goes to tax. Under the current tax system, you are in either of the 15, 28, or 33 percent federal tax brackets (ask your tax accountant). If your income decreases to the point that you drop into the lowest bracket, investments that save taxes probably are not beneficial. In other words, you would not save enough taxes to justify the added expense or lower return.

46

MEDICAID AND NURSING HOMES

Those who need skilled nursing home care but can't afford it may obtain assistance from Medicaid. The program is intended to help those with low incomes and modest assets. Therefore, to be eligible for assistance, both your income and personal wealth are subject to specified maximum limits. Because the program is administered by state level agencies, the rules vary depending on where you live. Still, some general guidelines can be offered.

Medicaid eligibility applies to individuals rather than couples. If you are married, income and assets can be divided between you and your spouse to determine qualification. However, if only one spouse requires assistance, you can't move all income and wealth to the other spouse. On the other hand, both spouses do not have to be destitute either. When one spouse enters a nursing home and the other remains at home, there are specific rules that determine how much income and assets the spouse at home can have.

Income. The spouse at home is entitled to receive a monthly maintenance needs allowance from the income of the nursing home resident spouse. In addition, a shelter allowance is included. The limits are set on a case-by-case basis, but federal law capped the total at $1500 per month in 1989—plus cost of living adjustments in later years.

Assets. A person needing nursing home care and having assets above the Medicaid limit, must use up the excess asset before becoming eligible for assistance. Certain assets that benefit the spouse may be protected. Those who are married may exempt the greater of $12,000 or one half of their combined life savings up to $60,000 plus a family home in which the spouse resides, other household goods, a car, and a burial and funeral fund for the spouse. It does not make any difference if assets are solely in the name of the spouse.

Unmarried individuals entering a nursing home face more severe limits. These vary by state but generally they may keep only $2,000 of savings, and there are dollar limits for categories of exempt assets.

Asset Transfers. There are limits on how a person applying for Medicaid can transfer assets (to children, for example) in order to become eligible. Any transfer occurring more than 30 months prior to application is exempt. If an asset is transferred for less than its market value within 30 months, the asset may have to be counted against the limit, as if the person still owned it. Transfers between spouses are not limited because the couple's assets are pooled to determine eligibility. Also, if the asset is a home, it can be transferred without penalty to the spouse, a child who has cared for the person for at least two years, a child dependent on the applicant, or a brother or sister having an equity interest in the home and having lived in the home for at least one year.

Transfers of assets to children are beneficial because they do qualify as transfers after 30 months. The parent should be careful to retain enough assets to get through the 30-month period with adequate cash flow.

Another strategy is to transfer assets into a Medicaid qualifying trust. Assets are put in a trust and beyond the elderly individual's control, though he or she receives the income during a lifetime. Once gifts are made they cannot be revoked. Transfers must be made more than 30 months before eligibility, for assets to be protected.

If any of these situations apply, see your local Medicaid office for more specifics. You may also want to consult with an estate planner or tax expert to determine the financial and tax consequences of any transfers or sales.

QUESTIONS AND ANSWERS

The following is a hypothetical conversation between a counselor on elderly housing (**C**) and a married couple (**MC**) contemplating retirement in a few years. It is offered to illustrate some of the important considerations in retirement planning.

MC: Maybe this visit is a bit premature, but we want to retire in a few years and need to think about where to live.

C: Certainly, it's not too early to begin thinking about your future. In fact, you should be making some concrete plans.

MC: What are some important factors in the decision?

C: Some obvious ones are:
- Where do you want to live?
- What lifestyle do you want to pursue?
- How much can you afford to spend?
- How much will your health affect what you can do?

MC: Suppose that we really want to live right here in the same two-story, four-bedroom home that we have been living in for more than 20 years.

C: That's fine. Most retirees do just that. You probably have many friends in the area and perhaps your children or other relatives live nearby. You are familiar with shopping, personal services, and medical care in the neighborhood. You know just about how much it will cost. Staying put may be a very reasonable choice. On the other hand, your old neighborhood may have changed for the worse and no longer be safe. Also, you may enjoy a milder climate or an atmosphere more conducive to the leisure lifestyle.

MC: What else might we consider in this decision?

C: The house sounds as if it will provide more space than you need. Consider the additional effort for cleaning and maintenance, and extra costs for utilities and property taxes. Also, the house has two stories. That may be fine for right now, but could pose a problem as you age, especially if all of the bathrooms and bedrooms are upstairs.

MC: What can we do about that?

C: Some remodeling might be helpful. You need not do anything now, because you're in good health. However, if something happens that makes climbing stairs or otherwise getting around especially difficult, you may need to remodel. You might also consider converting part of your home to an accessory apartment—something we'll discuss later.

MC: What types of remodeling changes might be helpful?

C: Perhaps you can add a bathroom downstairs—where the pantry now is—and convert the den or dining room to a bedroom.

MC: That sounds like a good idea—we always wanted a bathroom downstairs—why should we wait to get ill?

C: If you make changes now and then decide to sell the home for whatever reason, you lose the benefits of remodeling. In addition, your changes might even lower the value of your home to a prospective buyer, so you could get hit financially by a double whammy. In this case, an additional bath usually adds value to a home, so perhaps you should do it now—or whenever you're prepared to put up with the disruption of construction work in your home.

MC: What if we keep the home and do some traveling? A couple we know has an RV. They drive south in the winter and live in campground facilities.

C: Many people are "snow birds." They will find campgrounds catering to their needs and meet other retirees with similar lifestyles. There certainly is something to be said for avoiding the harsh winters we have here.

MC: If we sell, what other local housing choices do we have?

C: Plenty. You can buy another house nearby, more suitable to your needs, like a condominium or cooperative, or rent a house or apartment. Many of these need less maintenance, and you easily could come out with cash in the transaction. Some people move to their dream home when they retire because they then realize they can afford it; others move down in housing.

MC: If we buy a less expensive house, won't the profit on the sale of our old house become taxable? How much tax must we pay when we sell our house?

C: It could be none. The first $125,000 of gain from the sale of a house is tax exempt (the gain includes all the untaxed gains from other houses you have owned). To be eligible, you must have used the home as a principal residence for three of the last five years, and one of you must be at least age 55 when you sell it. You can do this only once in a lifetime.

MC: What kind of housing is available out of town?

C: If you want to move, find a community that you will enjoy, and buy a house or condo. It may be too expensive to be in the most exclusive suburbs of an expensive city, so look for a nice, affordable place. You might rent for a year or so before buying to get a feel for the area and decide whether you really want to move. If you like to be with people your age, there are some lovely retirement communities in the Sunbelt, especially Florida, Texas, Arizona, and Southern California. Many offer tennis courts, pools, golf courses, and lakes, and have shuffleboard, bridge games, and group activities on a regular basis. They are not necessarily expensive—two-bedroom units are available for under $100,000.

MC: We visited one—most people there seemed old to me.

C: Yes, but nearly all are still leading healthy, active lives. Besides, new arrivals will tend to be younger than those who have been there for a few years.

MC: What about the new law that says anyone can live anywhere? Could that mean a family with rowdy children could live next door?

C: Amendments to the Fair Housing Law do just that, but make exceptions for communities where nearly all residents are above a certain age.

MC: Can we rent condominiums in retirement communities?

C: Certainly! Many complexes have an active rental market. Some owners buy years in advance of their expected need and are happy to find a careful tenant during that time. Some spend only part of a year in their community and want to rent for the months that they are away.

MC: Can we afford these?

C: We haven't discussed finances yet. Now is a good time to talk about that.

MC: Upon retirement at age 65, Social Security will provide us about $1,500 per month. A company pension will pay us another $2,000 or so, mostly tax free. We have almost $50,000 in a bank CD that earns nearly 8 percent. A real estate broker says that we will clear at least $100,000 if we sell our home.

C: You are in an enviable position compared to many retirees. Still, both income and assets are limited. You will have to spend carefully and wisely. Any other obligations?

MC: Our children are married and have good jobs, so we have no major financial concerns.

C: Fine! Because your assets are under $600,000 you really won't need professional estate planning help, beyond making out a will and offering clear instructions on locating your assets.

Sounds like you could buy a retirement home for about $100,000 and incur no debt on it. That would be favorable and conservative. Your income will provide ample cash to live, including vacations and leisure activities, provided they are not extravagant. As an alternative you could buy a more expensive place and arrange a mortgage.

MC: How much could we afford?

C: Your income is about $3,900 per month, so you can spend at least a third of that, $1,300, on housing. Actually, some lenders allow you to qualify for a higher percentage, but let's just use $1,300, for example. Now subtract $200 for monthly utilities and $100 for maintenance, leaving $1,000 per month. That $1,000 must cover principal, interest, taxes, and insurance (PITI). Taxes and insurance vary widely, though about two percent of the house cost a year will cover them in most places. Interest rates are 10 percent a year, so your mortgage payments each year will be about 12 percent. That works out to payments of about one percent each month for PITI. With your $1,000 remaining housing allowance, you can borrow up to $100,000 on a mortgage.

With another $100,000 from the sale of your present home you can afford a maximum of about $200,000—of course, these amounts must be fine-tuned for the specific home and area.

MC: Should we spend that much for housing?

C: I would not recommend it, and suggest that you become debt free upon retirement. Paying a lender is one less worry. And be sure to keep ample liquidity, such as your CD, to be conservative. Besides, upon the death of either of you, Social Security payments will be reduced. Will you lose your pension income also?

MC: We think so—but there may be a large lump sum to collect if that happens soon after retirement.

What happens to people who take on large debts in retirement, then lose a major source of income?

C: Many have to sell or move to less expensive housing. But if their present house has appreciated in value, a reverse annuity mortgage or sale leaseback may be appropriate.

MC: What are reverse mortgages and sale leasebacks? Are they for us?

C: Probably not. They are for people who are house rich but have little or no income.

MC: How do reverse annuity mortgages work?

C: A lender agrees to make monthly payments to the borrower for a certain period of time. The amount is based on the home's value, the borrower's age, and how long the income will last. These payments from the lender to the borrower add to the debt, and are increased by compound interest.

MC: Could the debt exceed the property's value?

C: That could happen, though most programs allow the owner to continue living there without payments. Most of the reverse annuity mortgage programs are experimental, so they are not available everywhere or at all times.

MC: What about a sale leaseback?

C: You would sell your house to an investor and you would receive a cash down payment and the right to live in the house for as long as you desire. You would lend the buyer the rest of the money and receive payments on the loan. Those receipts would approximate the rent you'd have to pay the investor. Also, the buyer takes over the costs of maintenance and taxes.

MC: Why would we do that?

C: Perhaps to raise cash now, or to fix the price of a sale now or to avoid the aggravation of a sale later.

MC: Why would an investor do that?

C: Probably for the tax advantages of ownership and possible appreciation in the value of your home.

MC: We can use some more income on retirement—as can everyone—but we don't want to give up control of our house. What else can we do?

C: Perhaps you can convert part of your home into an apartment—called an accessory apartment—and lease it out. Home sharing can work if the parties are compatible.

MC: You mean another person or couple our age?

C: Yes, but the parties must be compatible—not necessarily the same age. In fact, you might find a much younger person or couple who could help with things around the house and look in on you as needed. Be sure to check the local housing and zoning codes to determine whether they allow such a conversion.

MC: We always thought that if we need help with everyday life, we could move in with our children.

C: Seems that now you and your children are independent and both households enjoy separate lifestyles. If you are compatible with your children, living together could be viable, especially if it becomes a necessity. If one, or both, of you becomes ill it would be nice to be close to children. It can be a good economic decision and a mutually beneficial arrangement. Many daughters-in-law couldn't or wouldn't work outside the house without grandma's help with housework and kids. Again, though, not all parties are compatible. You might become a great burden to them if your health deteriorates.

MC: We have heard of housing for the elderly whereby rents are really low—some can get a fine apartment for about half the rent charged locally.

C: There are government subsidized apartments for low-income elderly. Some offer a 20 percent discount—some others offer deeper discounts, depending on need. For example, one FHA program has the tenant pay market rent but no more than 30 percent of their income. For someone making $500 a month, rent would be only $150.

MC: We have friends who have difficulty leaving their house because of an age-related disability, but still live there. What will happen to us if our mobility deteriorates in the next few years?

C: You can stay in your home and have in-home help. You may be able to get a meal delivered each day, daily household help, and a physical therapist and doctor to visit as needed. There are agencies that can coordinate necessary services.

You can remodel to make access easier when using a walker or wheelchair, and put handrails in the bathrooms or halls. A therapist can help place these aids for maximum convenience.

If you can go outside, senior citizen centers can help exercise your body and mind, and offer companionship with others your age. Adult day care centers offer professional help, including assistance for those with severe impairments.

MC: What are continuing and life-care communities?

C: These are places that can increase housing and medical support as your needs increase. They generally are expensive. The entrance fee can exceed $100,000 and the monthly fee $1,000. Many are attached to a skilled nursing home and guarantee you a place if needed. Some guarantee care for the patient's entire life at no increase in fees, even when a nursing home is needed.

MC: What living arrangements are possible for those who are dependent on others for just about everything they need to do?

C: Choices are limited for those who are so dependent. Elderly people would be very fortunate to have a child tend to them, or to have a spouse who can take care of their needs. Care virtually is a 24-hour job, seven days a week. The relative must be extremely patient, caring, and devoted.

Another possibility is in-home foster care. Nurses, therapists, and housekeepers can be brought into an individual's home to provide around-the-clock services. Needless to say, costs are high. There are some foster homes that offer a family environment for the elderly, but these may be difficult to find and even more difficult to determine their quality level. Finally, there is the nursing home. There are different levels of care that may be offered even within the same building. Some residents may have extensive freedom and an enjoyable social setting. But for others, unfortunately, the atmosphere is too institutional. It may be difficult to get the individual personal attention, care, and privacy expected. Many feel that they literally are too restrained, frequently strapped into wheelchairs on the pretense that a patient might otherwise fall and cause self-injury.

MC: Is there anything else to think about?

C: Think about the lifestyle you'd enjoy, and how to achieve it. You should do some more financial planning, especially to understand your pension benefits. Perhaps you want to look into revising your medical coverage and disability benefits, or arranging long-term care insurance. See what other things you might be able to do to increase your retirement income. Please feel free to call or visit again whenever you wish.

MC: Thank you for your help. We have something to think and talk about.

GLOSSARY

Accessory apartment a completely separate living unit inside a single-family home. A potential source of care giving between an older person and neighbor, providing the convenience of physical closeness, while maintaining privacy. Provides additional income to the landlord and a low rent for the tenant.

Administration on Aging the principal agency in the federal government responsible for administering most provisions of the Older Americans Act. In the Office of Human Development Services, Department of Health and Human Services. It concentrates on the needs, concerns, and interests of older citizens.

Adult care providing facility refers to long-term care facilities, emergency shelters, boarding homes, and other congregate living arrangements.

Adult day care center provides activities for senior citizens that help maintain physical and mental well-being. Usually has trained staff to help those with physical or mental limitations.

Adult foster homes an adult care-providing facility, usually limited to a few residents, that emphasizes a family environment.

Aging network a system of federal, state, and local agencies, plus private organizations and institutions, responsible for serving or representing the needs of older people. The network is involved in developing service systems, advocacy, planning, research, coordination, policy development, training and education, administration, and direct service provision.

Alternate care facility a care facility that offers 24-hour-a-day supervision and sufficient support for frail older people with substantial functional limitations who do not need medical intervention. Less restrictive environment and less expensive than a nursing home, but provides more supervision than a continuing care facility.

Annuity a series of payments made at regular intervals over the lifetime of the recipient or for a predetermined period.

Assisted housing housing that receives financial assistance through a federal, state, or local program. The assistance can be an interest subsidy, rent subsidy or contributions toward capital costs. Assisted housing usually has a public benefit, such as for low- and moderate-income people.

Board and care home (also known as *domiciliary care, personal care, residential care*) a living arrangement that consists of either private or shared sleeping rooms and bathrooms, meals, and housekeeping. Some facilities provide supervision and selected personal care services.

Boarding home a living arrangement that usually consists of a bedroom-sitting room, private or shared bathroom, and meals served in a common dining area.

Care management programs designed to facilitate and coordinate service to older people with multiple or complex needs who may be assisted by several different service providers.

Circuit breakers a form of property tax relief in which the amount of relief depends on both personal income and the property tax bill. When property taxes exceed some percentage of income, the circuit breaker overrides the property tax levy and rebates the excess amount to the taxpayer.

Community-based care a term used to describe a wide range of noninstitutional services, including supportive, health, and personal care. These help older people maintain maximum, independent functioning in their homes or another environment of their choice. The community care network may include family, friends, religious institutions, and public and private agencies.

Condominium ownership of one's own dwelling and generally the land it is on, with shared ownership of common areas. Each dwelling can be mortgaged individually.

Congregate housing a generic term used to describe living arrangements for older people who need or want to live close to other people for socialization or assistance with activities of daily living. These facilities, which are called by many names, generally include a combination of private space for each resident, plus shared space and facilities or services.

Congregate services a package of services delivered to eligible frail older people living in selected senior housing projects. Helps to maintain independence and avoid institutionalization.

Continuing care a housing option in which the provider offers shelter and needed support services. Services can change as residents age and require additional kinds and levels of assistance, including skilled nursing care. *See also* Life Care.

Conventional rental (1) When referring to assisted housing, housing that receives no subsidies and is operated strictly on market terms. Tenants must pay whatever rents are charged and no other funds are available to cover operating expenses. (2) When referring to specialized housing such as congregate, housing that does not include special services or special design features, such as shared bath facilities.

Cooperative (co-op) housing residents are stockholders in a corporation that owns the building in which they live. Residents have occupancy rights for their individual units, rather than owning the units.

Deferred annuity a series of regular payments that begin after a specified period of time.

Deferred payment loan a loan where the borrower is not required to pay interest or principal until death, or the sale of the home. *See also* Reverse Annuity Mortgage.

ECHO (Elder Cottage Housing Opportunity) the system of putting a complete, small house temporarily on the same lot as a caring family. Allows access to informal support that enables an older person or couple to avoid institutionalization.

Health Care Financing Administration a branch of the U.S. Department of Health and Human Services concerned with the financing and delivery of health care to aged, disabled, and poor.

Home delivered meals *see* Meals on Wheels.

Home equity the value of a home, less any mortgage or other lien secured by the home.

Home equity conversion the process of borrowing against the equity one has built up in a home. *See also* Home Equity Loans, Reverse Annuity Mortgage.

Home equity loans the borrowing of money against the value of equity in one's home. Generally in the form of a second mortgage for either a home equity line of credit or a fixed amount for a fixed term.

Home Improvement Program a general term for any program that provides funds to improve existing single-family houses. Funds may come from a variety of sources, such as tax-exempt bonds or state appropriations, and may be used in different ways, such as loans or grants.

Homes for the aged a generic term for residential facilities designed for older people who need or want some kind of help or support with everyday activities.

Such homes provide, at a minimum, sleeping facilities, meals, and housekeeping. There is wide variation in the kind and amount of supervision, personal care, and supportive and rehabilitative services provided.

Home sharing/house matching a kind of shared housing arrangement in which two nonrelatives are matched to live together, share expenses and allow for mutual support and assistance. Usually sleeping quarters are private, and the rest of the home is shared.

In-home services or in-home foster care refers to home health aid, family respite services, visiting and telephone reassurance, and chore maintenance. These enable older people to remain in their homes for as long as possible.

Life care a kind of continuing care living arrangement in which the changing needs of residents as they age are met with additional kinds and levels of assistance. The distinction is sometimes made that life care guarantees shelter and services regardless of resident needs without increases in the agreed upon monthly fee. By contrast, continuing care also provides needed services but usually with an additional fee.

Life estate the right to lifetime residency.

Limited equity resale a restriction placed on a property, such as a cooperative apartment, at the initial purchase that sets a limit on the price at resale. It is used where the initial purchase price was reduced below actual market value, and is intended to assure continued affordability for future buyers.

Loan-to-value ratio the amount of a loan as compared to the value of the home that secures it.

Local Housing Authority the government body responsible for administering public housing subsidies at the local level. Housing authorities generally finance and manage public housing developments and administer Section 8 Existing Housing programs.

Long-term care a term used to represent a range of services that address the health, social, and personal care needs of individuals who have never developed or have lost some capacity for self-care. Services may be continuous or intermittent, but it generally is presumed that they will be delivered indefinitely to people who have a demonstrated need.

Long-term care facility a skilled nursing facility, intermediate care facility, nursing home, and any other similar adult care home.

Long-term care insurance insurance that typically pays a certain amount per day, such as $50 or $100, if the insured needs to enter a skilled care home or similar facility. May have a maximum policy payout limit, such as $200,000.

Meals on Wheels a program authorized under the Older Americans Act that provides at least one home delivered hot or other appropriate meal per day, five or more days a week. Serves older people who are homebound or for whom congregate meal facilities are not accessible.

Medicaid assistance program for the financially needy. A joint federal/state program that provides medical assistance for the aged, blind, disabled, and families with dependent children who cannot pay for medical care by themselves. Benefits vary among the states.

Medicare provides medical benefits to those over age 65. Part A is hospital insurance. All retired workers qualified to receive Social Security benefits, and their dependents, qualify for hospital insurance. Payroll taxes on employers and workers fund this. Part B, supplementary insurance, is optional. It provides additional coverage to pay for physicians' services. Coverage also is available for those who are under age 65 and have been receiving Social Security disability benefits for 24 consecutive months.

Mortgage any instrument that creates a lien against real estate as security for the payment of a debt.

Nursing home a type of long-term care facility that provides intensive supervision by staff, which often is medically skilled.

Old-Age, Survivors and Disability Insurance (Social Security) the basic program of cash payments to workers when earnings stop because of retirement, death, or disability. OASDI is financed by Social Security contributions from employers and employees.

Ombudsman an official or representative appointed to receive and investigate reported complaints. Reports findings, and helps bring about equitable solutions. Every State Unit on Aging provides this service directly or by contract.

Property tax deferral programs that permit older people to delay paying some or all of their property taxes until either death or property sale. Generally, below-market interest rates are charged on the amount deferred.

Property tax freeze a local program that freezes an older home owner's property taxes in recognition of the owner's limited or fixed income.

Property tax relief programs to reduce the burden of property taxes on lower-income households. Includes homestead and circuit breaker programs, renters' credits and deductions, tax deferral, and property tax freezes.

Remainder interest the right to occupy and/or sell a home and receive all proceeds after the life estate has ended.

Remodeling or renovation for accessibility installing ramps, handrails, and adaptive devices in the bathroom and kitchen to accommodate a wheelchair or walker. Enables a handicapped senior to continue living at home for an extended length of time.

Rental Assistance (Subsidy) Program a program that provides funds toward rental payments required to be paid by qualified tenants. A variety of federal and state programs currently are in use, with varying regulations governing eligibility.

Renter credits and deductions states may credit renters with a percentage of rent paid. Usually the programs apply to people of all ages and income groups, but some state programs provide greater benefits to low-income and older age groups. Most programs have a maximum income eligibility.

Residential care facility a living arrangement for frail older people who need some assistance with activities of daily living. The "care" component consists of various kinds and levels of services and support. *See also* Alternate Care Facility.

Retirement community housing developments designed for and marketed to healthy older people. Units usually are for sale, although some may be for rent. Recreation facilities and social activities typically are available. In some retirement communities, certain supportive services are offered for a fee.

Reverse annuity mortgage the borrower receives income for a period of time or life, or a lump sum amount. Borrower does not need to make a payment until the house is sold, or death. The home is pledged as security.

Rooming house a living arrangement that consists of a bedroom-sitting room and private or shared bathroom. Meals may or may not be provided.

Sale leaseback the sale of a home to a buyer who immediately leases it back to the seller.

Senior citizen center a community or neighborhood facility that provides a broad spectrum of supportive services for older local residents. May include health, social, nutritional, and educational services, and offer recreational facilities.

Service access programs that link or connect the elderly to services they need.

Shared housing *see* Adult Foster Homes, Home sharing, House matching.
Skilled care homes a type of long-term care facility that provides continuous supervision by skilled medical staff.
State Housing Finance Agency (HFA) an agency created to make mortgage funds available for housing, either single family or multi-family. Funding comes primarily from issuance of bonds. Mortgages are targeted to certain segments of the state population.
State supplement state programs of cash payments to needy individuals to purchase care in a residential facility. The concept is to fund or create the service and provide the means to purchase the service for individuals who might otherwise choose a nursing home.
State Unit on Aging an agency of state government designated by the governor and state legislature as the focal point for all matters related to the needs of older persons within the state.
Supplemental Security Income (SSI) a cash payment program for needy aged, blind, and disabled people, financed from general revenues by federal and state government.
U.S. Department of Health and Human Services Federal agency that regulates and funds a variety of health, income maintenance, and human services programs. Includes Social Security, Medicare, Medicaid, and Aid to Families with Dependent Children.
U.S. Department of Housing and Urban Development federal agency that regulates and funds a variety of programs, including housing programs.

Source: Portions adapted with permission from *State Initiatives in Elderly Housing,* Council of State Housing Agencies, National Association of State Units on Aging, Washington, D.C.

CHECKLIST

PART I: Considerations Applicable to All Types of Retirement Housing

The Neighborhood, The Community

Physical Characteristics of Immediate Neighborhood

_____ Residential atmosphere
  _____ clean
  _____ not too crowded
  _____ not too noisy
  _____ well maintained
_____ Fairly level terrain; easily negotiated in all weather
_____ Free of smoke and air pollution
_____ No heavy traffic; well-marked crosswalks
_____ Well-paved
_____ Well-lighted streets and sidewalks
_____ Curbs six inches or less in height
_____ Adequate sewerage and drainage

Basic Community Services

_____ Effectively policed
_____ Fire station in the vicinity (20 blocks or less)
_____ Post Office within two to three blocks; mail delivery to housing facility
_____ Public transportation within one block
  _____ regular
  _____ frequent
  _____ early
  _____ late evening

_____ to downtown areas
_____ to planes, bus, and train terminals

Basic Commercial Facilities and Services Nearby

_____ Shopping
  _____ within two to three short blocks of housing development
  _____ no heavy traffic routes to cross
_____ Choice of stores for necessities
  _____ groceries
  _____ variety, notions, stationery
  _____ medications and drugs
  _____ clothing
  _____ hardware
_____ Beauty parlor
_____ Barber shop
_____ Restaurants
_____ Hot meals delivered to home
_____ Laundry facilities
_____ Dry cleaning
_____ Tailor shop
_____ Shoe repair
_____ Bank
_____ Maintenance and repair services available (particularly important for home owners and apartment dwellers)
  _____ plumber
  _____ electrician
  _____ painter
  _____ carpenter
  _____ roofer
  _____ TV repair
  _____ locksmith
  _____ janitorial work, such as heavy cleaning, yard care

Facilities, Programs, Opportunities: Religious, Cultural, Social, Educational, Recreational

- _____ Places of worship within walking distance
- _____ Special activity and service programs for older adults within walking distance, sponsored by
  - _____ activity center for older persons
  - _____ community centers
  - _____ church or synagogue
  - _____ civic organizations
  - _____ unions
  - _____ fraternal organizations
- _____ Public Departments of Recreation, Parks, Adult Education
- _____ Opportunities for volunteer services
- _____ Museums
- _____ Commercial entertainment: movies, concerts, plays, sports

Health Facilities, Programs, and Services Available

- _____ Hospital
- _____ Regular physical checkups, diagnosis, and treatment available through
  - _____ private physician
  - _____ dentist
  - _____ podiatrist
  - _____ oculist
  - _____ ear specialist
  - _____ clinic
- _____ Health and hospital insurance plans
- _____ Visiting nurse services
- _____ Rehabilitation, occupational and physical therapy services
- _____ Home for the aged
- _____ Nursing home
- _____ Ambulance service

Social Service Agencies and Programs Available

_____ Central information and referral services through

  _____ Community Health and Welfare Councils
  _____ Departments of Health
  _____ Departments of Welfare
  _____ Public Housing Authority
  _____ Private Family Agency

_____ Professional casework and counseling services: help with

  _____ personal and family problems
  _____ budget and home management
  _____ employment
  _____ financial assistance

_____ Home help services

  _____ homemaker and housekeeping services
  _____ friendly visiting
  _____ visiting nurse
  _____ home delivery of meals
  _____ shoppers service

Employment Opportunities, Full- or Part-Time

_____ Job counseling
_____ Training
_____ Placement agencies

The Housing Facility

Sponsorship: Stability, Responsibility

If profit motivated

_____ fairly large corporation, more than three-person ownership
_____ financially sound
_____ experienced in housing for older people

If nonprofit

_____ backed by organization with large membership to rely on for support

Exterior Features

_____ Relatively level site

  _____ easy access in and out

_____ Attractive landscaping

  _____ outdoor sitting areas

  _____ privacy

_____ Well-lighted

  _____ policed

  _____ well-maintained

_____ All stairs or terraces with guardrails

_____ Adequate sewerage and drainage

_____ Ample parking space for visitors

Structure and Design

_____ Entrance

  _____ no or few steps and with guardrails

  _____ covered

  _____ well-lighted

_____ Sound construction

  _____ fireproof and protected with fire alarms

  _____ safety devices easily accessible

_____ Nonskid floors

_____ Interior steps with guardrails

_____ Corridors wide and well-lighted

_____ Doorways to living quarters wide enough for pass through of furniture or wheelchairs

_____ Elevators for building with two or more stories

_____ Ample dead storage space

_____ Laundry facilities accessible, preferably not in basement

The Living Unit

_____ Designed for privacy

  _____ soundproof

_____ Spacious and furnishable

  _____ cheerful, pleasant, airy

_____ Enough light

  _____ ventilation

_____ Ample closet space

_____ Electrical equipment appropriate for safety and convenience

  _____ light switches placed at room entrance and within the room to permit lighted path to and from any part of quarters

  _____ electrical outlets sufficient in number and at proper height to avoid long dangling cords

  _____ enough electric current to permit simultaneous use of modern appliances

_____ Individual heating controls in living quarters

_____ Windows

  _____ low enough to see out of from sitting position

  _____ safe to operate and clean

  _____ properly shaded to avoid glare especially from large expanse of glass

_____ Enough water pressure

• The Bathroom:

  _____ large enough to move around in and accommodate wheelchairs

  _____ distance from lavatory to opposite wall sufficient to permit full stretching of legs or for just dressing properly in case of leg or hip fracture

  _____ heavy-duty anchored towel racks and grab bars appropriately placed

_____ bathtub low enough for easy access and easy cleaning

  _____ nonskid bottom

  _____ seat ledge for soaking feet or to sit while taking shower

_____ faucets placed so that water temperature can be controlled *before* showering or bathing

  _____ recessed soap dishes

_____ ample medicine and storage cabinets at appropriate height

_____ adequate ventilation

_____ alarm system in case of emergency

_____ clothes rack for drying personal laundry

• The Sleeping Area:

_____ separate bedroom or

  _____ separate alcove that can be shut off for privacy

  _____ with window not blocked by outside wall

_____ space around side of bed

  _____ place for nightstand, night-light and phone near bed

  _____ uncluttered path from bed to bathroom, if possible

• The Living Area:

_____ layout and wall space allowing furniture placement without cluttering floor area

_____ enough space to work, view TV, read, write, entertain a few guests without needing to ship furniture

• The Kitchen: (see Part II, Housekeeping Living Arrangements, page 132)

Programs, Facilities, Services Available on Premises

_____ Chapel
_____ Library
_____ Community center or clubhouse
_____ Social lounges
_____ Card and game rooms
_____ Arts and crafts
_____ Opportunities to serve as volunteers
_____ Outdoor recreation facilities
_____ Garden plots for tenants use
_____ If private transportation
    _____ frequent
    _____ regular
    _____ late return pickup
_____ Optional dining facilities
_____ Tenant mutual help arrangements
_____ Employment opportunities
_____ Professional staff
    _____ social worker
    _____ program director

Health and Social Service Arrangements on Premises

_____ Infirmary
_____ Medical center
_____ Doctor
_____ Registered nurse

If infirmary or medical center, is it
    _____ licensed by state
    _____ supervised by doctor
    _____ supervised by registered nurse

If not on premises, in event of short-term, acute, or long-term illness, are there definite arrangements with hospital and other agencies in the community?

_____ Yes

_____ No

_____ Group health, hospital, nursing home insurance coverage through the housing facility

_____ Intercom system in case of emergency

_____ Professional social worker to help with personal and family problems

Costs

Regardless of type of living arrangement, get careful breakdown of costs: what is included, what is extra. (See checklists for each type of living arrangement.)

If founders' fees, life lease contracts, membership fees, life care are the method of payment, answers to the following questions are essential:

1. What actually is in the payment—occupancy only, occupancy and certain services? What is included in monthly charges?
2. What happens if housing operation is unsuccessful? Will provisions be made for occupancy under same terms elsewhere? Will proportionate amount of the funds be returned, depending on length of stay and cost of services consumed?
3. What happens if the resident has to move? Will the same refund arrangements be enforced?

Reasons for Termination of Occupancy

_____ Changes in health

_____ Inability to care for apartment

_____ Family situation

_____ Specific length of absence

_____ Nonpayment of rent over a specific period of time

Waiting List

Is it necessary to pay a reservation fee to be put on a waiting list?

_____ Yes

_____ No

What has been rate of turnover during last three years?

If operation is new, what are chances for application?

PART II: Special Checklist for Housekeeping Living Arrangements

Kitchen

_____ Has sufficient space for efficient preparation of meals

_____ eating

_____ working

_____ Window permits looking out when seated and eating

_____ Counter space sufficient, low enough to work at while sitting down

_____ Cabinets sufficient for storage and at appropriate height to avoid undue stooping, stretching, climbing

_____ Appliances low enough for easy access and use

_____ Double sink to permit hand laundry as well as dish washing

_____ Refrigerator with freezer section not too low and small

_____ Range with oven
if electric

_____ with signal light when in use
if gas,
_____ with automatic shut off control

Rental Housekeeping Apartments

Length of Lease

_____ One year
_____ Two years or more, (if life lease, see Part I, Costs, page 131)

Costs

_____ Maximum rent, exclusive of services is no more than 30 percent of individual's annual income

Monthly Rent Includes

_____ Utilities
_____ Heavy cleaning and maintenance service

Monthly Payment Expected in Advance

_____ First month
_____ First and last month
_____ One year

Extra Charges

_____ Parking
_____ Recreational and other activities
_____ Health and social services
_____ Membership fee

Other

If one member of couple is left alone
_____ will he need to change to smaller apartment?
_____ will he be able to retain same apartment but at lower rent?

Housekeeping Cottages or Apartments to Purchase (Cooperative, Condominium, or Individual Home Ownership)

_____ Total price of living accommodations is no more than 2½ times family's annual income
_____ Amount of initial down payment
_____ The amount of monthly payments include
    _____ mortgage amortization
    _____ payment on principal and interest
_____ Maintenance cost of common facilities
_____ Other fixed charges
    _____ utilities
    _____ taxes and assessments
    _____ comprehensive home insurance
    _____ heating
    _____ upkeep
_____ Fees for closing of sale
    _____ attorney's fee
    _____ title search or insurance
    _____ filing
    _____ other
_____ Services and equipment included in cost
    _____ garage
    _____ parking
    _____ awning, screens, storm windows
_____ Kitchen appliances
    _____ range
    _____ refrigerator
    _____ freezer
    _____ dishwasher
    _____ garbage disposal
_____ Laundry appliances
_____ Shades
_____ Draperies
_____ Carpeting
_____ Upkeep and maintenance of

_____ grounds
_____ recreation facilities
_____ exterior of buildings

_____ Privileges of using recreational facilities, clubhouse or center and other facilities
_____ private bus
_____ other services

_____ Health insurance plan

Part III:
Special Checklist for Nonhousekeeping Residence Club Hotel-type Living Arrangements

Physical Features of the Building: Cheerful, air, clean, well-maintained, soundproof

Fire Safety

_____ Fire safe building
_____ sprinkler system in rooms, corridors, lounges
_____ fire alarms, hoses, and extinguishers on each floor

_____ Handrails in corridors

Living Quarters

_____ Private, spacious, and furnishable room and bath, which meet general specifications in Part I

_____ If room is shared, is it to be no more than two persons?
_____ Yes
_____ No

Is is large enough for privacy?
_____ Yes
_____ No

Is there an opportunity to change room if resident cannot get along with roommate?

_____ Yes
_____ No
If bathroom is shared, by how many?
How far from living unit?

_____ Hot plates in room or community kitchens for preparing snacks

_____ Intercom system or switchboard with someone on duty 24 hours

_____ Telephones private
_____ through switchboard

_____ Furnishings provided
_____ completely
_____ partially
_____ not at all

_____ Resident can do personal laundry in room

Costs

What services are included in monthly rate (if founders' fees, life lease, life care)

_____ maid service; linen service, how frequently
_____ room service
_____ other

Management Policies: Services

Meals Policies

_____ Dining hours fixed
_____ 1 hour per meal
_____ 2 hours per meal

_____ Hot meals delivered to rooms when necessary

_____ Menus
_____ family style
_____ multiple-choice
_____ special diets prepared and honored

Absence Policies

Is payment required while resident is away, for

_____ meals
_____ cleaning
_____ linen

How much notice is required to receive credit?

Do charges continue indefinitely if an emergency prevents giving adequate notice?

If one member of a couple is left, will he be moved to a smaller room?

Provisions for Returning Late at Night

_____ Resident given keys to outside entrance
_____ 24-hour doorman
_____ Night watchman
_____ Other arrangement for getting in after facility is closed

What Happens When Resident is Ill

If doctor or nurse are in residence, are they available or on call for night emergencies?

_____ Yes
_____ No

If infirmary is on premises, is it

_____ licensed by state
_____ supervised by doctor
_____ supervised by registered nurse

Can resident call infirmary directly in case of emergency at night?

_____ Yes
_____ No

Arrangements with community hospital for serious illness?

_____ Yes
_____ No

Arrangements with nursing home for long-term illness?

_____ Yes
_____ No

_____ Room service, shopping services available for the ill

_____ Drug prescriptions taken to be filled for resident

Commercial Hotel Services

In addition to above considerations, does hotel provide

_____ bellhops
_____ switchboard
_____ room service
_____ activities and other programs (See Part I)

Source: Portions adapted with permission from *A National Directory on Housing for Older People,* pages 213–222, prepared by the National Council on Aging, Washington, D.C.

DIRECTORY OF STATE UNITS ON AGING

Alabama Commission on Aging
136 Catoma Street
Montgomery, AL 36130 (205) 261-5743

Older Alaskans Commission
Department of Administration
P.O. Box C
Juneau, AK 99811-0209 (907) 465-3250

Arizona Aging and Adult Administration
Department of Economic Security
1400 West Washington
Phoenix, AZ 85007 (602) 542-4446

Arkansas Division of Aging and Adult Services
P.O. Box 1437 Slot 1412
Little Rock, AR 72203-1437 (501) 682-2441

California Department of Aging
1600 K Street
Sacramento, CA 95814 (916) 322-5290

Colorado Aging and Adult Services Division
Department of Social Services
1575 Sherman Street - 10th Floor
Denver, CO 80203-1714 (303) 866-3851

Connecticut Department on Aging
175 Main Street
Hartford, CT 06106 (203) 566-3238

Delaware Division of Aging
Department of Health and Social Services
1901 North DuPont Highway
CT Building, 2nd Floor
New Castle, DE 19720 (302) 421-6791

District of Columbia Office on Aging
1424 K Street, N.W. - 2nd Floor
Washington, DC 20005 (202) 724-5626

Florida Aging and Adult Services Program Office
Department of Health and Rehabilitation Services
1317 Winewood Boulevard
Tallahassee, FL 32399-0700 (904) 488-8922

Georgia Office of Aging
878 Peachtree Street, N.E.
Room 632
Atlanta, GA 30309 (404) 894-5333

Guam Public Health and Social Services
Government of Guam
Agana, Guam 96910

Hawaii Executive Office on Aging
Office of the Governor
335 Merchant Street - Room 241
Honolulu, HI 96813 (808) 548-2593

Idaho Office on Aging
Statehouse - Room 108
Boise, ID 83720 (208) 334-3833

Illinois Department on Aging
421 East Capitol Avenue
Springfield, IL 62701 (217) 785-2870

Indiana Department of Aging and
Community Services
P.O. Box 7083
Indianapolis, IN 46207-7083 (317) 232-7006

Iowa Department of Elder Affairs
Jewett Building - Suite 236
914 Grand Avenue
Des Moines, IA 50319 (515) 281-5187

Kansas Department on Aging
Docking State Office Building
915 S.W. Harrison - Room 122-S
Topeka, KS 66612-1500 (913) 296-4986

Kentucky Division for Aging Services
Cabinet of Human Resources
CHR Building - 6th Floor
275 East Main Street
Frankfort, KY 40621 (502) 564-6930

Louisiana Office of Elderly Affairs
P.O. Box 80374
Baton Rouge, LA 70806 (504) 925-1700

Bureau of Elder & Adult Services
Department of Human Services
State House - Station 11
Augusta, ME 04333 (207) 289-2561

Maryland Office on Aging
State Office Building - Room 1004
301 West Preston Street
Baltimore, MD 21201 (301) 225-1100

Massachusetts Executive Office of Elder Affairs
38 Chauancy Street
Boston, MA 02111 (617) 727-7750

Michigan Office of Services to the Aging
P.O. Box 30026
Lansing, MI 48909 (517) 373-8230

Minnesota Board on Aging
Human Services Building
444 Lafayette Road
St. Paul, MN 55155-3843 (612) 296-2544

Mississippi Council on Aging
421 West Pascagoula
Jackson, MS 39203 (601) 949-2070

Missouri Division on Aging
2701 West Main
Jefferson City, MO 65102 (314) 751-3082

Montana Governor's Office on Aging
Capitol Station
Helena, MT 59620 (406) 444-3111

Nebraska Department on Aging
301 Centennial Mall - South
P.O. Box 95044
Lincoln, NE 68509 (402) 471-2306

Nevada Division on Aging
1665 Hot Springs Road
Suite 158
Carson City, NV 89710 (702) 885-4210

New Hampshire Division of Elderly & Adult Services
6 Hazen Drive
Concord, NH 03301 (603) 271-4680

New Jersey Division on Aging
Department of Community Affairs
CN 807
Trenton, NJ 08625 (609) 292-4833

New Mexico State Agency on Aging
La Villa Rivera Building - 4th Floor
224 East Palace Avenue
Santa Fe, NM 87501 (505) 827-7640

New York State Office for the Aging
Empire State Plaza
Agency Building No. 2
Albany, NY 12223 (518) 474-4425

North Carolina Division on Aging
Taylor Hall
693 Palmer Drive
Raleigh, NC 27603 (919) 733-3983

North Dakota Aging Services
Department of Human Services
600 East Boulevard Avenue
Bismarck, ND 58505 (701) 224-2577

Northern Mariana Islands Office of Aging
Department of Community and Cultural Affairs
Civic Center - Susupe
Siapan, Northern Mariana Islands 96950
Tel. Nos. 9411 or 9732

Ohio Department on Aging
50 West Broad Street - 9th Floor
Columbus, OH 43215 (614) 466-5500

Oklahoma Special Unit on Aging
Department of Human Services
P.O. Box 25352
Oklahoma City, OK 73125 (405) 521-2281

Oklahoma Department of Human Services
Aging Services Division
312 N.E. 28th Street
Oklahoma City, OK 73105 (405) 521-2327

Oregon Senior Services Division
313 Public Service Building
Salem, OR 97310 (503) 378-4728

Pennsylvania Department of Aging
231 State Street
Harrisburg, PA 17101-1195 (717) 783-1550

Puerto Rico Gericulture Commission
Department of Social Services
P.O. Box 11398
Santurce, PR 00910

Rhode Island Department of
Elderly Affairs
160 Pine Street
Providence, RI 02903 (401) 277-2858

Territorial Administration on Aging
Office of the Governor
Pago Pago, American Samoa 96799 011 (684) 633-1252

South Carolina Council on Aging
1 Greystone West
240 Stoneridge Drive - Suite 207
The Midlands, SC 29210 (803) 758-2576

South Dakota Office of Adult Services and Aging
700 Governor's Drive
Pierre, SD 57501-2291 (605) 773-3656

Tennessee Commission on Aging
706 Church Street, Suite 201
Nashville, TN 37243-0860 (615) 741-2056

Texas Department on Aging
P.O. Box 12786 - Capitol Station
1949 IH 35-South
Austin, TX 78711 (512) 444-2727

TIPI Office of Elderly Program
Community Development Division
Government of TIPI
Saipan, Mariana Islands 96950
Tel. Nos. 9335 or 9336

Utah Division of Aging and Adult Services
Department of Social Services
120 North 200 West, Suite 401
Salt Lake City, UT 84103 (801) 538-3910

Vermont Office on Aging & Disabilities
103 South Main Street
Waterbury, VT 05676 (802) 241-2400

Virgin Islands Commission on Aging
6F Havensight Mall-Charlotte Amalie
St. Thomas, Virgin Islands 00801 (809) 774-5884

Virginia Department on Aging
700 E Franklin Street, 10th Floor
Richmond, VA 23219 (804) 225-2271

Washington State Bureau of Aging and Adult Services
Department of Social and Health Services
OB-44A
Olympia, WA 98504 (206) 586-3768

West Virginia Commission on Aging
Holly Grove - State Capitol
Charleston, WV 25305 (304) 348-3317

Wisconsin Bureau of Aging
Division of Community Services
One West Wilson Street
P.O. Box 7851
Madison, WI 53707-7851 (608) 266-2536

Wyoming Commission on Aging
Hathaway Building - Room 139
Cheyenne, WY 82002-0710 (307) 777-7986

STATE AGENCIES WITH CERTIFICATION PROGRAMS FOR CONTINUING CARE COMMUNITIES

Arizona Department of Insurance
3030 N 3rd Street, Suite 1100
Phoenix, AZ 85012 (602) 255-5995

California Department of Social Services
744 P Street - Room 1740
Sacramento, CA 95814 (916) 445-2077

Colorado Division of Insurance
Department of Regulatory Agencies
303 West Colfax, Suite 500
Denver, CO 80204 (303) 620-4300

Florida State Treasurer and Insurance Commissioner
The Capital Plaza - Suite 11
Tallahassee, FL 32399-0300 (904) 488-3440

Indiana Securities Commission of the Secretary of State
1 North Capitol - Suite 560
Indianapolis, IN 46204 (317) 232-6681

Kansas Department of Insurance
420 Southwest 9th Street
Topeka, KS 66612 (913) 296-3071

Michigan Department of Commerce
525 West Ottawa Street
P.O. Box 30004 - Law Building
Lansing, MI 48909 (517) 373-1820

Minnesota Department of Commerce
500 Metro Square Building
133 East 7th Street
St. Paul, MN 55101 (612) 296-4026

Missouri Division of Insurance
P.O. Box 690
Jefferson City, MO 65102 (314) 751-4126

Pennsylvania Insurance Department
1321 Strawberry Square
Harrisburg, PA 17120 (717) 787-2317

Texas Department of Human Services
701 West 51st Street
Austin, TX 78751 (512) 450-3011

Virginia Bureau of Insurance
P.O. Box 1157
Richmond, VA 23209 (804) 786-3741

Wisconsin Department of Insurance
P.O. Box 7930
Madison, WI 53707 (608) 266-3285

INDEX

Making the most of your maturity...

Barron's Keys to Retirement Planning
User-friendly manuals offer advice on many aspects of mature living. Each book is paperback, approximately 160 pages, $5.95, Canada $6.95.

Keys to Fitness Over Fifty *by Jo Murphy.* Inspiration and advice on exercises, relaxation techniques, dealing with stress, plus reasons for feeling positive about aging. (4514-9)

Keys to Buying a Retirement Home *by Jack P. Friedman, Ph.D. and Jack C. Harris, Ph.D.* Two real estate experts tell how to select the type of community and style of home that best suits your lifestyle and physical needs. (4476-2)

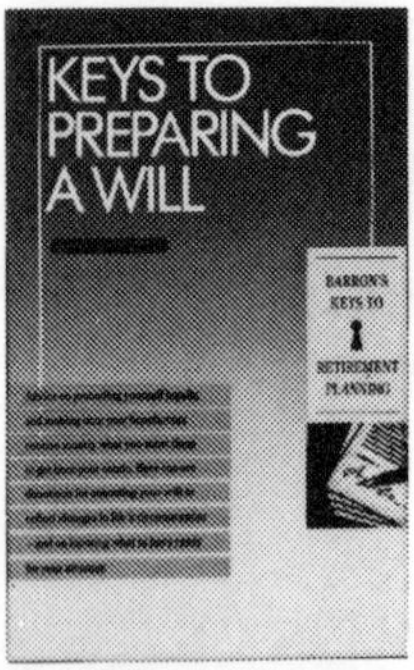

Keys to Preparing a Will *by James Jurinski* How to be sure your heirs receive your bequest according to your intentions. (4594-7)

Plus a comprehensive single volume of friendly general advice...

Life Begins At 50: *A Handbook for Creative Retirement Planning by Leonard Hansen.* Tips on retirement living, including handling your money prudently, knowing about available health care, Social Security and Medicare benefits, finding fun and bargains in travel and entertainment. Paperback, 352 pages, $11.95, Canada $15.95. (4329-4)

BARRON'S

BARRON'S EDUCATIONAL SERIES, INC.
250 Wireless Blvd., Hauppauge, N.Y. 11788
Canada: Georgetown Book Warehouse
34 Armstrong Ave., Georgetown, Ontario L7G 4R9

ISBN Prefix: 0-8120
Prices subject to change without notice. Books may be purchased at your bookstore, or by mail from Barron's. Enclose check or money order for total amount plus sales tax where applicable and 10% for postage & handling (minimum charge of $1.75, Canada $2.00). All books are paperback editions.

Printed in the United States
20473LVS00003B/109-144

9 781413 727197

The Keeper of the Key

By Mary Ann Wilcox

PublishAmerica
Baltimore

First printing

ISBN: 1-4137-2719-0
PUBLISHED BY PUBLISHAMERICA, LLLP
www.publishamerica.com
Baltimore

Printed in the United States of America

I would like to thank Lana Shawver for all her hard work proof reading my book by dedicating this book to her.

Mary Ann Wilcox
Oct. 20, 05

Prologue

Darkness was surrounding them, as not even one ray of light was visible in their prison. Why had they been so foolish as to come back to this forbidden place of darkness? Everything had happened so fast that they were totally unprepared for the events that had taken place so quickly.

Why had they come back a second time, when they had escaped unharmed the night before? Was it the lure of the locked door? Was it just being too stubborn, knowing all along that they shouldn't have ever come back to this place?

How long would it be before they were missed? Maybe days if the hurricane outside of their prison kept raging. How foolish they had been to not tell another person about the secret room and long maze of tunnels that connected this place with the inn. Now they were in this place all alone, wishing that someone knew they were there.

How long had they been locked in this place of darkness? Hours? Days? Time seemed to have no meaning as the two of them sat huddled together in their chamber prison. Surely they would perish, as the wind and rain tried with all of its fury to enter the walls of their hidden prison—walls that would surely collapse, burying them forever with their secret, a secret known only by them and THE KEEPER OF THE KEY....

Chapter 1

As Donnie made her way down from the huge red bus, she suddenly felt as if she were making a huge mistake by leaving its safety. A sudden chill seemed to enter her body, even though a warm breeze greeted her as she stepped into the soft sand that seemed to cover everything as far as she could see.

Soon all three pieces of Donnie's luggage were sitting beside her as she stood watching the last glimpse of the red bus disappear from sight, taking with it the only refuge there seemed to be on this now deserted highway.

Why am I standing out here alone? Donnie was starting to wonder. *Why isn't there someone here to meet me?*

Surely her grandmother had gotten her letter telling her that she was taking the summer job at her inn, the Jamaican Inn. In fact, her grandmother had nearly begged her to take the job at the inn for the summer—a job that was going to be more of a vacation than actual work, a job that was taking her to an island that seemed more like Jamaica in the 1890s than a Florida Keys Island in the year 2004. What had the letter said?

Dear Donnie,

I need someone to help at the inn all summer tutoring a young boy that lives here on the island. His father is a widower, and he can't seem to get over the loss of his wife long enough to attend to the needs of his young son. I know that you teach all year and need

a break, but teaching one small boy here on Cedar Key Island would still be a vacation. He would only need you a few hours a day, leaving you most afternoons, nights and of course your weekends free. Please come. This boy needs you.

Granny Kelley

Where can she be? thought Donnie as she picked up her suitcases and headed for the one lone bench that stood out in the middle of nowhere.

Some bus stop, she thought as she started looking around for a place where she could phone the Jamaican Inn, soon realizing that she was wasting her time.

Pulling out her cell phone now, Donnie realized that wouldn't help her either, as she tried to turn it on and found that it was no longer charged up.

"What have I gotten myself into?" Donnie mumbled as a sudden gust of wind tossed her short black hair and sent yet another chill shooting down the back of her neck. A small knot was slowly starting to form in the pit of her stomach—a knot that always seemed to be followed by an event that she didn't always enjoy.

"Stop all of this foolishness," Donnie scolded herself as the knot once again gnawed at her.

Looking down the highway once more, Donnie knew that she couldn't have missed anyone that had come to pick her up. The island was only accessible by the bridge that stood only a few feet from her and a private airstrip. Of course a person could go in by boat, but she knew that her grandmother never picked her guests up in that manner.

So why was she sitting out here alone waiting for a ride?

Of course Donnie had never come to the island by bus before, so she hadn't expected to find such an isolated spot on this side of the bridge. Now she knew that once she crossed the bridge, isolation could be found easily if a person desired it.

Donnie had always loved the Victorian village where the inn was, with its raw, natural beauty, where she had spent so many summers as she grew up. It had been five years since her last visit, and she hoped that this visit would be as splendid a memory as the years before.

Donnie was beginning to wonder if she might not regret this vacation as darkness was beginning to close in around her.

Now Donnie wasn't one that felt uneasy when darkness takes over, but as it descended on her suddenly, she felt as if the knot in her stomach was growing by leaps and bounds.

"Well, no more waiting for me," Donnie said as she started to juggle her luggage into her arms and making her way toward the bridge in almost total darkness now, not knowing what terrible fate awaited her.

A quietness seemed to close in all around Donnie as the fog slowly began to seep through the railing that separated her and the great body of water that seemed to stretch out into nothingness.

Donnie didn't ever remember feeling more alone in her life, as she hurried across the fog covered bridge hoping with every step that her grandmother would show up and make the feeling of helplessness go away.

Before long, the suitcases became so heavy that Donnie seemed to be struggling with every step that she took.

Surely I must have filled them with bricks, instead of my clothes and a few books for my soon-to-be student, she thought as her arms began to ache as she tried to make it just a few more steps.

Finding that she couldn't go another step, Donnie stopped for just a few minutes to rest. Setting her suitcases on the side of the walkway, she noticed that the fog had descended completely now, making it impossible to see even a few inches ahead of her.

Donnie was starting to wonder if it had been such a good idea to start for the inn. Maybe her grandmother had known that the fog was coming and had the good sense to wait until it lifted to cross the bridge.

"Why didn't I wait?" she asked. But she already knew the answer to that question.

She never could wait for anyone or anything, and this wasn't the first time that she had wished she had waited and didn't.

What was it Mother called me? Her little impatient bird, she thought.

Impatient or not, Donnie couldn't stay on this bridge the rest of the night. She had chosen to cross, and that's what she intended to do.

Before she could even picked up one piece of her luggage, a small flash of light appeared out of the fog.

At first the lights were so dim that Donnie thought that undoubtedly she must be seeing things, but the longer she stared into the mist the closer the lights came.

My grandmother has finally come for me, she thought.

"Here I am," Donnie shouted as the oncoming lights now blinded her.

"Turn your lights down," she yelled as she shaded her eyes.

Yet the car just kept coming, gaining speed, as it seemed to be heading straight toward Donnie. A scream tried to escape from deep inside of Donnie as she realized the speeding car was heading directly for her.

Don't they see me? she thought as she tried with every ounce

of strength left in her to move.

But she felt as if she were frozen to the spot where she now stood. Her legs felt like rubber.

Why is this happening to me? she thought. *Why didn't I stay on the other side of the bridge?*

Chapter 2

"Granny Kelly, come quickly!" Rodney shouted as he rushed into the Jamaican Inn trying to be careful with the motionless bundle that he carried.

"What's all of this noise out here at this time of night?" Granny Kelly asked as she hurried in from the kitchen, wiping sticky dough from her hands. "Can't a person get anything done in peace around here?

"Oh, it's only you Rodney Atwater. What's all this fussing about, and can't you shut the door when you enter a place?" Granny scolded as she crossed the shiny wooden floor of the lobby, not noticing that Rodney had his arms full.

"You didn't see any sign of my granddaughter or Hank's green station wagon, did you? I can't understand where they can be. Now, what's all this rushing and shouting you're doing?" Granny Kelly asked as she shut the door and turned back toward Rodney.

For an instant, Granny Kelly just stared at the unmoving figure that filled the large sinewy arms of the tall, muscular man that stood in the middle of the room. Realizing now what he was holding, she hurried over toward him on legs that almost gave way under her.

"Oh, Donnie," came her shaky voice as she tried to hold back the tears. "How did this happen?" asked Granny as she now looked at Rodney for the answer. "Where did you find my granddaughter?"

"Your granddaughter?" Rodney questioned as he went on

to explain what had taken place only moments before.

"I was out checking my fishing lines along the bridge, and there she was standing in the middle of the bridge with a car heading straight for her. That's when I pulled her out of the car's path and she fell, striking her head on the side of the walkway. She hasn't opened her eyes once. Don't you think we should call Doc Phillips?" Rodney said tenderly as his dark blue eyes showed the concern that he was feeling for the stranger that he held so very close to him.

"Let's take her upstairs first, and I'll clean her up some. If she still isn't any better after that, we'll see if we can locate Doc. However, that might be hard to do since I haven't seen him at breakfast for the last two or three days. You know how he gets when he's in the mood to fish. Nobody can find him for days. Probably out somewhere in this crazy fog in that silly old boat of his right now," said Granny as she looked at Donnie.

"Come on, let's take Donnie upstairs. I can't understand what happened to Hank," Granny said as she started up the spiral staircase. "I will never forgive myself if Donnie doesn't come out of this. I should have gone for her myself, but I thought Hank had changed and that he could handle one little thing, like picking up my granddaughter. I guess I was wrong," she said shaking her head as she continued up the stairs followed by Rodney.

"We'll put her in her own bed, and that way maybe she'll be a little more comfortable. If that's possible with the shape she's in," said Granny.

Very gently Rodney climbed the stairs that led to the second floor of the inn as Granny Kelly led the way down the long hallway, trying to avoid the squeaky spots in the floor, but with each step she or Rodney took, the floor seemed to squeak.

Not a sound could be heard from behind the closed doors of

Granny's guests as they passed. *Besides, it's well after midnight, and everyone is surely asleep by now*, thought Granny as they headed down the hall.

At the far end of the hall, Granny Kelly and Rodney turned and went down another small hallway that led to a single door. Granny opened it and stood back as Rodney entered with the still motionless Donnie.

"Lay her over here, Rodney," said Granny Kelly. "I knew I shouldn't have trusted Hank to pick her up. That man doesn't know what the word 'responsibility' means. You just wait until I see him tomorrow," mumbled Granny as she crossed the room.

As carefully as possible, Rodney placed Donnie on the soft feather mattress of the pink and white canopied bed that stood in the middle of an all pink and white room. Donnie moaned slightly as she sank slowly down into the soft feathers, almost being swallowed by the huge mattress.

As Rodney helped Granny remove Donnie' torn sandals, he couldn't keep from staring at her beautiful creamy white skin.

Such a beautiful face, he thought as he noticed a dark purple mark starting to appear on her right cheek—the cheek that had struck the walkway as he pulled her to safety. *What a cute little nose*, he thought as he had a sudden urge to place a soft kiss right on the tip of it.

What nonsense, he thought, as he realized how foolish that might look to the small woman that stood beside him trying to take care of her granddaughter.

"Stay here with her while I get something to clean her cuts and scrapes with," Granny Kelly said as she hurried from the room.

As Rodney watched Donnie breathing evenly now, he noticed she seemed to be resting better. He felt the need to know more about this newest addition to the island—an addition

that for some reason, Hank had tried to run down. He was sure that the green station wagon that had been on the bridge earlier was Hank's. He knew that the old man was odd, but he didn't know how odd until now.

He wouldn't say anything to Granny Kelly, and as soon as possible, he was going to have a little talk with the eccentric Hank and find out just what this newest craziness was all about.

Tomorrow he would make a trip to the lighthouse in the cove and confront Hank.

What if she never opened her eyes again? he thought. *How could I ever forgive Hank for this new foolishness? Well, tomorrow I'll take care of Hank*, he thought as he stood staring at the unmoving Donnie.

"I see she still hasn't moved," Granny Kelly said as she returned carrying a pan of water, bandages and some ointment to help her clean Donnie's wounds. "Why don't you go down to the kitchen and fix us both a strong cup of coffee? I don't know about you, but this has been a long night, and I need something to give me a boost. Now go on," Granny said as she saw how worried Rodney looked. "You can't do anymore for her right now, and the coffee will help us both," Granny said as she waited for him to leave.

Twenty minutes later, Rodney made his way back upstairs, carrying two steaming cups of coffee. As he entered the room, Donnie's grandmother nearly knocked the cups from his hands, trying to hurry him over to see what Donnie had done while he was gone.

"She's trying to open her eyes," Granny Kelly said excitedly.

Rodney set the cups on the small, round, white table that sat in the far corner of the room and crossed the room quickly. Donnie now lay under a pink and white striped sheet and seemed to be trying to open her eyes. She still didn't make a sound,

other than a small whimper once in a while. As Rodney moved closer, Donnie suddenly shot straight up, screaming over and over. Grabbing her instantly, Rodney held her tightly as she tried to pull herself free.

Pain seemed to be in every part of her body, as Donnie clung tightly to the strange arms that seemed to be there to protect her. Slowly, she felt the arms start to release her, but Donnie still clung, not wanting to let go.

Remaining still for a few moments longer, Donnie finally moved from the arms that seemed to belong around her. As she reluctantly lay back, her heart skipped a beat as she looked into the angelic face of the stranger sitting beside her. The pounding of her heart quickened as he spoke her name, trying to assure herself that she was safe now.

Safe from what, she thought as she tried to speak, but her voice didn't seem to be there, as she tried to clear the fog that cluttered her mind.

"Donnie, can't you speak?" came a familiar voice from the other side of her.

"Granny Kelly, what am I doing here?" Donnie said as she tried once more to sit up.

"Just lay quietly," Granny Kelly said as she reached over and gave Donnie a big kiss that stung as her lips touched Donnie's cheek.

As the cobwebs began to clear, Donnie realized that she was lying in a bed where she had slept many times on her summer vacations as a girl growing up. The walls were different now, all covered with pink and white roses, but the white and pink furniture scattered around the room was the same. Everything else in the room was the same as when she was little, except the tall figure that stood looking out her window at the ocean. *Where did he come from, and why does my heart*

pound so hard as I look at him?

He turned and looked into her eyes. "I hope you're feeling better. You had quite a nasty fall, a couple of hours ago," the stranger said as he neared her bed.

"Fall? I don't remember any fall," Donnie said. "How did I get here? The last thing I remember is crossing the bridge in the fog and lights that seemed to blind me."

"You were almost killed," Granny Kelly answered. "Rodney saved your life."

So that's my knight's name, thought Donnie. *Sir Rodney,* she thought, as she tried to keep her eyes off of him.

"What do you mean killed?" Donnie suddenly asked as she realized what Granny Kelly had said.

"Dead and all because you were stupid enough to stand in the middle of the road, on a fog covered bridge. Don't you know better than to pull a stunt like that?" came the now harsh voice of Rodney. "You should have waited for someone to pick you up!"

"I was tired of waiting for a ride. I wasn't about to spend the night at that deserted bus stop!" Donnie shouted back in a tone that let her knight in shining armor know that she didn't like his attitude.

"Well, you certainly don't walk down the middle of a bridge in the fog at night," yelled Rodney.

"I'll walk wherever I like, and it's none of your business," Donnie shouted again.

"Next time I'll let you get hit by a speeding car!" shouted Rodney as he crossed the room toward the door.

"Stop this," Granny Kelly said as she stepped between Donnie and the now fleeing Rodney.

"You may not be grateful, but I am grateful to Rodney. He saved your life."

"Well, I am not grateful to this rude, outspoken creature," said Donnie. "I want him out of here or I'm going," yelled Donnie as she struggled to her feet, the pain nearly making her fall. Pushing the hands of Rodney from her arm as he tried to catch her, Donnie made her way toward the door.

My protector indeed, she thought as she reached the bedroom door, wanting to get as far away as possible from this rude person that even now caused a strange sensation and a pounding in her heart.

Donnie entered the narrow hallway quickly, not wanting to be caught by the two interfering people that were yelling for her to come back. *Come back to what?* she asked herself.

"No way am I going back in that room to be treated like a baby," she yelled. "No way!" Donnie said as she hurried down the narrow hallway.

Almost to the main hallway now, Donnie suddenly stopped as she realized she wasn't alone. Not two feet from her stood a figure dressed all in black, with its back toward her. She stood frozen holding her breath, hoping that if she kept quiet, the strange figure might just go away. But the sound of the door opening behind her caused the figure to turn suddenly for just a second and stare right at Donnie with eyes so blue that she felt that she could almost see into its very soul.

Realizing that others were about to enter the hallway, the figure in black suddenly turned and darted around the corner. Moving quickly Donnie tried to follow the mysterious figure, but before she could enter the main hallway, a door slammed in the distance, and as she rounded the corner, the hallway stood empty.

Why was this mysterious figure in the entrance of my room? asked Donnie herself as she stood listening for a sound. *Had he been listening to what had been going on between Granny*

Kelly, Rodney and me? But why? thought Donnie.

What a strange place, she thought as she listened once again, trying to hear a sound—a sound that might tell her which door the strange person in black had disappeared into. *What kind of a job have I gotten myself into?* she wondered as she made her way down the long hallway toward the stairway.

A job that seemed to be filled with nothing but strange people and danger at every turn….

Chapter 3

As Donnie arrived at the end of the hall, she paused for a moment, listening for some kind of a movement from behind one of the closed doors. All was quiet. Whoever had been listening to the argument moments before now stood behind one of the closed doors hoping that she hadn't discovered which room he or she now occupied.

Donnie didn't know how long she stood listening, but she soon decided that she was wasting her time hoping that the unknown person would make a move.

Reaching now for the banister, she slowly moved down the stairs. She knew if she lingered much longer she would have to face that rude Rodney Atwater again, and she had had enough of him for one night.

As she descended the stairs, Donnie suddenly came face-to-face with yet another unfamiliar person. Coming up the stairs toward her, dressed in a yellow-flowered housecoat, was a short, slightly heavy girl wearing glasses that were ready to slide off the end of her nose. This new addition was carrying a cup with steam coming from it, and looking up only at the last second, she almost spilled the contents of the cup as she ran right into Donnie.

"Oh, I' m sorry. I didn't know anyone else was up at this late hour," the strange girl said as she pushed her glasses back on her nose, trying to get a better look at Donnie.

Donnie tried to hurry past her, not being in the mood to meet yet another new person tonight. However as she tried to

squeeze by, this new person stuck out her small, almost child-like hand, and said "Hi, I am Julie Howell. I am one of the maids here," she said, her voice almost a whisper now.

Not taking her hand, Donnie quickly mumbled a slight hello and her name, hoping she could get this over quickly.

"Oh, you're Mrs. Kelly's granddaughter—the one that's going to tutor Mark Turner. He is such a sweet little boy," she said as Donnie tried to escape down the staircase.

"Well, I see you two have met," said Granny Kelly as she appeared at the top of the stairs, followed by the one person that Donnie didn't want to be near again tonight. "Why don't we move this noisy group down to the kitchen?" she said as she took both girls by an arm and headed down toward the main floor. "I don't think my guests will appreciate being disturbed at this hour."

Once they reached the main floor, Granny turned the group to the left and started to enter a large green and yellow door, but before they could step inside, a door slammed behind them, making all three of them turn to see who was leaving. Looking around, they soon figured out that Rodney had fled the inn, and not very happily.

Well, so what, thought Donnie as Granny looked first at the closed door and then at her.

As the girls followed Granny through the green and yellow door, they found themselves in a large dining room filled with round, white tables, all surrounded by small wicker chairs.

Following on across this beautiful room, the girls entered another door at the far end of the room. Once inside, they found themselves standing at the end of a large kitchen—a kitchen that Donnie remembered sitting in many years before having hot chocolate and peanut butter cookies.

"Now you two sit over there and get to know each other,"

said Granny as she crossed the kitchen to a set of yellow cabinets.

Julie and Donnie headed for a small wooden table and chairs that stood at the other end of the room. Not a word passed between them as they watched Granny Kelly busily making hot chocolate.

"Well, you two are sure a talkative pair tonight," replied Granny as she placed the steaming cups in front of the two girls along with a plate of peanut butter cookies. "You weren't short on words just a little while ago. In fact, I would say you had a little too much to say to a certain young man."

"I don't care to talk about any of this right now," answered Donnie as she turned a light shade of red, as Julie's ears seemed to perk up at the tone in her voice. "In fact I'm taking my hot chocolate and cookies to my room, where I can eat them in peace," came the almost rude tone again as Donnie moved across the kitchen and out the door, leaving Julie and Granny Kelly staring at the closed door.

As Donnie walked quickly through the dining room, she felt that silly knot starting to form in the pit of her stomach again—the same knot that she had felt on the bridge earlier.

Oh, stop being silly, she told herself as she entered a now dark lobby.

Weren't the lights on earlier? thought Donnie as she tried to make her way to the staircase.

Suddenly a cold chill made its way up the back of her neck as Donnie tried to feel her way through the darkness toward the stairs. Carefully feeling the banister, she made her way up one step at a time. Then, suddenly, as she reached the top, out of the darkness came a pair of gloved hands that gave Donnie a gentle shove—a shove just hard enough to send her plunging down into the darkness at the bottom of the stairs.

* * * * *

Falling through the darkness for the second time in less than six hours, Donnie lay sprawled out on the last two steps of the staircase. Too stunned to move or even call out, she lay and watched as the lights came on. People seemed to be coming from all directions. Her head seemed to be spinning as she tried to lift it and couldn't.

"Stay still," came a voice from above her. "Don't try to move," Donnie heard someone saying as she opened her eyes to find herself staring into the palest blue eyes she had ever seen—the eyes of yet another stranger.

"Oh, Donnie, are you all right?" shouted Granny Kelly rushing from the kitchen, closely followed by Julie.

"I…I'm fine," Donnie managed to say as she tried to sit up, feeling so foolish with all of these strangers staring at her sprawled on the stairs.

"She must have tripped in the darkness and fell," said the blond-haired man kneeling beside Donnie.

She started to tell them that she didn't trip, but before she could even speak, the front door of the inn flew open, and there staring down at her was the one person she didn't want to see right now.

"You sure spend a lot of your time on the ground," came the snappy voice of Rodney as he stood over her now.

"No, I don't usually spend a lot of time on the ground, but for some reason, people on this island seem to enjoy knocking me there!" shouted Donnie as she suddenly pulled herself from the hands of the handsome blue-eyed man that kneeled beside her.

As she struggled to her feet, both men tried to grab her, as her knees almost gave out form under her.

"Back off," yelled Donnie as she pushed them both away. "I

can manage to get myself up those stairs without your help" she said as she pushed her way through the small crowd that had gathered at the top of the stairs.

Looking back once as she made her way down the hall, Donnie saw that both men were watching from the spot where she had just left them.

What's Rodney doing back here anyway? He always seems to be turning up whenever I manage to take a fall, thought Donnie as she neared her room.

Two falls in one night, and he was around both times. A knight in shining armor or the stranger in the dark, she thought as she entered her room.

Once inside, Donnie all but fell into her bed. She leaned back against the pillows trying to get into a comfortable position. Her already bruised and sore body was once again starting to throb with pain. If she could get out of bed in the morning, she would be surprised.

She needed something for the pain as she tried to pull herself up from the bed.

"Stay put," said Granny Kelly as she entered the room, followed by Julie. "Haven't you fallen enough for one day? Now stay in that bed and take these pills so you can get some rest. I'll sit here until you fall asleep, just like I did when you were my sweet little angel," said Granny as she motioned for Julie to leave them alone.

Donnie jerked as the door clicked shut. She had had enough for one day.

"Sh, sh, it's alright," Granny whispered as she rubbed Donnie's bruised and swollen hands. "Just lay back and close you eyes. I am here now, and no one can hurt you anymore tonight," said Granny Kelly, as Donnie seemed to relax and start to drift off.

Moving slowly to the door, Granny took one last look at the sleeping Donnie, hoping that she would stay put for the rest of the night, and quietly left the room.

As Granny Kelly closed the door, Donnie opened her eyes for only a second.

Some vacation, thought Donnie as she slowly drifted back into a deep sleep. Two falls in one night, and she knew for sure that the last one was no accident.

Why is someone trying to get rid of me, and why is that Rodney person always around when it happens? she thought as she drifted back into a deep sleep....

Chapter 4

As the morning sun came through the window of Donnie's room, she tried not to open her eyes. Moving carefully, she sat up feeling the pain of her aching muscles from the night before. Falling twice in one night had not been kind to her.

If I had any sense at all, I would be on the next bus home, thought Donnie as she made her way to the large bathroom at the far end of her room. "Maybe a good hot bath will make me feel better," she said to the bruised and tired looking face that stared back at her from the mirror that hung on the rose-colored walls of her bathroom.

Soon steam began to fill the room as the hot water flowed into the light pink tub that stood on claw feet in the middle of the room. Removing her robe was even a painful ordeal, and as Donnie slipped slowly down into the hot tub, her many scrapes and bruises stung with so much pain that she soon had tears spilling from her eyes. Sitting there with tears running down her cheeks, Donnie once again felt a sudden urge to leave the inn at once and return to the safety of her small apartment back in Illinois.

"Don't be silly," she scolded herself as she reached for a pink-flowered towel to dry herself. Donnie knew that she couldn't leave Cedar Key Island and the inn until she knew who wanted to harm her or run her home.

Running a brush through her short hair, Donnie smiled at the image that now appeared before her. Dressed in a blue blouse and white shorts, Donnie felt that she was ready to start her

day. Except for the scrapes and bruises, she looked like any vacationer ready for a day at the beach.

Reaching for her new sandals, Donnie shook her head as she looked at the now ruined sandals. The strap had broken when she was almost hit by that car on the bridge last night. This trip was sure taking a toll on her.

Now what am I going to wear for shoes? she thought as she pulled out her suitcase. Inside she found a light blue pair of anklets and a pair of white tennis shoes. Feeling the pain as she tied the laces across her bruised left foot, Donnie wished her sandals weren't ruined, as the tennis shoes seemed to dig into her skin.

Hobbling down the long hallway toward the main staircase, Donnie stopped as she stood at the top looking down the well-lighted carpeted staircase. She could almost see herself lying at the bottom after being pushed.

Last night, when her mind was in such a daze, she wasn't sure that she had been pushed, but today with a clear head Donnie was sure that someone had reached out of the darkness and shoved her. Looking behind her, a sudden chill seemed to run up and down her spine as she felt as though someone was near, watching her.

Was the mysterious man in black listening behind one of the closed doors behind her? Without waiting another second, Donnie hurried down the stairs nearly running over Julie at the bottom.

"Oh, I'm sorry," Donnie said as she stopped.

"Where are you off to in such a hurry?" asked Julie as she stepped out of Donnie's way.

"I thought I would get a cup of coffee before I took my first walk on the beach."

"Forget any coffee for now," Julie said. "I just came from

the kitchen, and Granny Kelly is in one of her moods trying to get things ready to feed the guests. It will be a while before breakfast, and I don't think I would ask her for even a cup of coffee. I wouldn't mind a walk on the beach myself, if you don't mind some company," Julie said as she started for the front door. "I can't clean any of the rooms until after breakfast."

"No, I wouldn't mind some company," Donnie lied. She had hoped to spend some time alone sorting out the events that had taken place in the last 24 hours, but she knew how rude it would have sounded to say it out loud. Instead, she followed Julie quietly out the front door.

Without a word passing between them, they headed off to the right of the inn, soon coming to a path that Julie started down. Following her slowly, Donnie was starting to wonder if a walk was such a good idea as the pain in her left foot seemed to be throbbing more and more with each step. As they continued down the path, the beach below soon came into view, and before long Donnie and Julie stood beside the huge blue water just taking in the breathtaking view.

Without a word passing between them, they started up the beach, passing through a gap of rocks. Beyond the entrance stood a small, red, wooden bridge leading to an island that held an old lighthouse.

Crossing the bridge, Donnie saw the top of the Seahorse Lighthouse that stood on the top of a steep, sandy hill. The lighthouse was almost hidden by the trees that had grown up around it over time.

As they climbed the hill, Donnie noticed how worn the old lighthouse looked. It was in need of a paint job, and she wondered why it had been neglected with so many visitors coming to the island each year. It was almost like it was being kept this way to keep people away.

Stepping closer, Donnie wondered what the inside might be like. Circling around toward the back, she soon found a door that looked in much better shape than the rest of the structure. In fact, it looked like a door that was only a few years old. *Too modern to be the original one*, she thought as she reached for the doorknob.

"Get away from there, you two," came a gruff voice from the left side of Donnie.

But before she could utter one sound, she found herself, once again, begin pushed to the ground and looking up into the face of an old man with eyes so wild looking that Donnie was sure he was going to strike her dead before she could even defend herself.

As Donnie looked passed the wild-eyed old man, all she could see of Julie were her pink shorts and well-tanned legs as she ran back up the beach. *Just great,* she thought as she realized that now she was alone with a crazy old man standing over her with no hope of escape. *Some way to be treated*, she thought as she saw Julie disappear through the rocks where they had entered earlier.

"I knew there would be trouble when I heard you were coming, and right away I find you snooping where you don't belong," yelled the old man.

"But I was just going to look inside the lighthouse," Donnie managed to get out.

"That's the problem. No one is allowed in the lighthouse," said the gruff old man as he put his face right next to Donnie's face. "NO ONE!" he shouted as Donnie lay there wondering what he did to people that tried to enter the old lighthouse.

Why did I ever come to this island? Donnie wanted to shout as she started to look for a way to escape the wrath of the crazy old man that towered over her.

But an escape seemed impossible, and any help from Julie was out of the question because she was no where in sight. *Why, oh why, did I come to this place?* thought Donnie as she stared into the eyes of the wild old man….

Chapter 5

"Stop, Stop," came the welcomed cry of a voice that seemed to belong to a person who was always near these days when Donnie was in danger.

Looking away for a second, Donnie saw Rodney running through the rocks, followed closely by Julie. Looking back at the old man for a moment, she saw that his eyes were filled with such anger that she feared he would turn on her before Rodney could stop him.

"Hank, leave her alone," Rodney yelled as he came to a stop right at Donnie's head.

"She's messing with things that she shouldn't," shouted Hank as he pointed a long thin finger in her face.

"Don't worry about her, Hank. She's new on the island. She doesn't know that no one goes near the old lighthouse, except you. I'll talk to her and make her understand," Rodney said as he led Hank away from where Donnie lay. Donnie was too afraid to move, fearing if she did that the crazy old man would turn on her again.

"Are you alright?" said Julie in a low shaky voice as she reached down and helped Donnie to her feet.

"I thought you had run out on me," Donnie said as she tried to brush the dirt and sand from her white shorts.

"I would never do a thing like that," Julie said with a hurt look in her eyes. " I wouldn't run out on you. Honest. I just knew we needed help, and I knew Rodney should be at his fishing lines this time of morning. I knew we needed help right

away with that crazy old Hank."

Donnie still didn't say a word as she continued to inspect the new damage to her already battered body. With so many bruised places already, it was hard to spot any new damage. But she knew there had to be some.

" I should have told you that we stay away from this old lighthouse, but I never dreamed you would try to open a door, and before I could say a word, Hank had already knocked you to the ground. I am really sorry," Julie said, pushing her glasses back up her nose.

"You sure spend a lot of time on the ground," Rodney said in a rather snappy tone as he returned alone, the strange Hank no where in sight.

"No, I don't usually spend a great deal of my time on the ground, but on this island people seem to enjoy knocking me there," Donnie said as she stared into those beautiful eyes. She felt her knees go a little weak, as he seemed to almost take her breath away and she quickly looked away. "What's with that old man anyway?" she managed to say as she tried not to look at those beautiful eyes again. "I really thought he was going to hurt me before you came to help me."

"He's just strange. Stay away from the old lighthouse, and he won't bother you again," Rodney said in an even harsher voice as he started off toward the rocks.

"Anyway, Julie should have known better than to bring you down here," said Rodney as he hurried back up the path.

"Wait," Donnie yelled. "I want to at least say thanks for helping me." But he was already heading through the opening between the rocks, acting like he didn't hear a word she was saying. "Well, he is one of the rudest men I have ever met," Donnie mumbled to herself forgetting that Julie was still standing behind her.

"He's not really like that at all. He spends a lot of his time alone tending his fishing lines, and that makes a person forget their manners sometimes," Julie said as Donnie turned around.

"I still think he's one of the rudest men alive, and I hope he stays out of my way," Donnie said as she stormed off up the beach leaving Julie standing alone by the lighthouse.

"Talk about rude people," Julie yelled as she ran passed Donnie. "See if I save you again from a crazy old man or anyone else!"

"Wait," Donnie, shouted as she tried to run after Julie, almost falling as she felt the pain again in her left foot. She had been so worried about Rodney that she had completely forgotten about Julie going for help. "Wait," she yelled again, but Julie was already out of sight.

What a place! It's even turned me into a rude, uncaring person that can't even thank a friend for saving me from a crazy old man.

Making her way over and sitting on the edge of the bridge, Donnie took her tennis shoe off to look at her now bleeding foot. Knowing that it was a long walk back to the inn, Donnie knew that there was no way she could walk with her shoe rubbing the already bleeding foot. Taking off her other shoe, she began the long walk back. Walking across the bridge was easy, but once she stepped into the sand, Donnie had trouble keeping the sand out of her bleeding foot.

"At this rate it will be night time before I can get back," she said to a crab that was slowly making its way toward the water.

Hunger was starting to set in too. The last thing that Donnie had eaten was a burger and fries at one of the stops the bus had made yesterday around noon. She had planned to eat the cookies that her granny gave her last night, but the fall on the way to her room had taken care of those. Almost limping now, she

finally came to the path that led back up to the inn.

Maybe if I rest for a few minutes, I can make it the rest of the way, she thought, sitting on a large boulder that sat at the edge of the path.

Looking toward the ocean, Donnie noticed a small boy and a man running and playing at the edge of the water. At once she realized that the boy must be Mark, the boy she was to tutor.

Beside him was the handsome man from her fall last night. He towered over the small boy, and his shoulders were well-developed and tanned to a golden brown. Last night he had looked at her with the palest blue eyes, and suddenly she could feel those same eyes staring at her now.

Running ahead of the man, the small boy was heading right for her. As he neared her, Donnie saw that he had the same blond hair and pale blue eyes as the man behind him.

"You must be the new teacher," said the boy as he reached Donnie.

"And you must be Mark," Donnie said as she reached down and tousled his blond hair.

"How are you feeling today?" asked the man behind Mark.

"Better I thought," Donnie answered looking down at her foot.

"Let me have a look at that," the man said taking her foot in his hand.

"Is she alright, Dad?" Mark asked as he moved closer to see what his father was looking at.

"By the way, I'm Mark's father, Terry Lancing," he said as he put her foot back down. "Last night you rushed off so fast that I couldn't introduce myself."

"I am sorry that I acted like such an idiot last night," Donnie said. "I had just had enough of Rodney Atwater for one night."

"Rodney's not such a bad guy," Terry said. "He's just alone

a lot of the time. He spends too much time with his fish."

"I don't really care what he does with his time," Donnie said as she hopped down from her perch.

Seeing the fire in her eyes at the mention of Rodney's name, Terry knew that he was better off not talking about the subject anymore.

"I need to get back," Donnie said as she started to limp up the path, but before she could take even one step, she felt herself being lifted from the spot where she stood.

"Just relax," Terry said as he settled Donnie in his arms. "It will be a lot faster if I just carry you up the path," he said as he started toward the inn.

Reaching the inn, Terry set Donnie on the top step of the porch of the inn.

"Thank you, Terry," said Donnie. "I don't think I would have made it back before dark if you and Mark hadn't come along."

"Just don't try to take anymore walks for a while. Your foot needs to heal first," said Terry. "Mark and I are going in for lunch. Would you care to join us?"

"Sure, if you think they will serve a woman without any shoes," Donnie laughed as she stood and headed for the front door. "I might have a little pull with the cook," she said as Mark and Terry followed her inside.

Entering the dining room, Donnie saw that most of the tables were full. Her grandmother was clearing a table and putting the dirty dishes in a large green pan on a cart behind her.

"Donnie, where have you been?" asked Granny Kelly as she looked down at her bare feet.

"I took a walk, and now I can't wear my shoes," she said as Mark and Terry came up behind them.

"In fact, if Terry hadn't helped me back, I might still be stuck down by the beach."

"You three just sit here, and I'll fix you right up," Granny said as she finished wiping the table. "Do you want a menu or should I surprise you?"

"Oh, surprise us," Mark said as he bounced into the chair next to Donnie.

As Donnie looked around the dining room, she noticed another stranger staring at her. As their eyes met, he looked away quickly, giving Donnie a sudden chill.

"That's Doc Phillips," Terry said as Donnie turned her attention back to the two men at her table. "He is very strange at times, but he is handy to have around when you need a doctor."

"Does he stay here at the inn?'" asked Donnie, as she once again caught the strange doctor staring at her.

"In fact, maybe he should look at your foot," said Terry rising from his chair.

"Wait," Donnie tried to say, but it was already too late, as Terry hurried across the room.

"Doc Phillips, I want you to meet Donnie," Terry said as he returned with the doctor at his heels.

"Nice to meet you," he said as he pulled up a chair. Terry said you have a foot that needs looking at," he said as he moved closer.

"It's really nothing," Donnie said as she tried to avoid the doctor's touch.

"Let him look at you," Granny Kelly said as she pulled a small cart filled with food behind her.

Putting her foot into the coarse hand of Doc Phillips, Donnie waited while he turned it over looking at the sand and dirt covered wound.

"It's not really bad. But you need to clean it and keep those tennis shoes off of it. What were you doing out on it anyway?"

Doc asked as Donnie turned to the food that Granny was sitting in front of her, not answering the question, hoping that she could avoid any question about her walk.

The food seemed to disappear almost instantly, as Donnie seemed to inhale it.

"Slow down. No one is going to steal it from you, Donnie," said Granny Kelly as she watched the hungry girl barely stopping between bites.

Seeing that Donnie was no longer interested in talking about her walk, Doc Phillips rose and left the trio without even a word.

"A little more coffee," Granny Kelly asked as she made her way around to the few guests that lingered after lunch.

"No, Granny I've had enough for now. Besides I need to get my little friend here started on his studies," Donnie said as she stood. "Meet you on the back patio in five minutes, Mark," Donnie said as she headed for the door.

"Can you get upstairs alright," asked Terry as he hurried behind her.

"I'm fine now," Donnie answered. "Thanks for all of your help. I don't think I could have made it back without the help," she said as she made her way to the stairs.

Reaching the top of the staircase, Donnie turned to see Terry watching her. It was kind of nice having someone watching over her. Waving to him, she smiled and started down the hallway toward her room.

As soon as Donnie entered her room she knew that something was wrong. Looking around, she couldn't seem to put her finger on what was causing the strange feeling that she had, but she knew something wasn't right in her room.

Searching for a clue, Donnie entered her bathroom carefully, not knowing what or who might await her inside the doorway.

Was the person from last night hiding inside, waiting to once again attack her? Knowing that she could regret her decision to enter the bathroom, Donnie quickly stepped inside. Her heart was pounding so hard that surely her attacker would hear the loud beating and sense the fear she was feeling if he was waiting to harm her. A fear that was in fact giving her the strength to go on into the unknown danger that might still linger somewhere near her.

Switching on the light, Donnie quickly looked around.

At first, she saw nothing. Then she saw it. She was now face-to-face with the latest attempt to make her flee the island of Cedar Key.

Holding her hand over her mouth now, trying to hold back a scream, all she could do was stand and stare at this new danger….

Chapter 6

"Leave before it's too late!!!"

That was the message that was now scribbled on the mirror that Donnie stood facing. All Donnie could do was stand and stare at the letters that warned her to leave.

Who was doing these awful things to her and why? Did she know something that she wasn't aware of? But how could she know something? All of this had started even before she set foot on the island.

Shaking now, Donnie looked around for something that she could remove the warning with before Granny or someone else could see it. She didn't know how she wanted to handle this latest development, but she didn't want anyone else to know about it. In fact, as soon as she could talk to Julie, Donnie would make sure that she didn't mention the events at the lighthouse either. Whoever was doing this had to be able to move around the inn with ease, she decided. It had to be someone that knew she was coming and was afraid that she would discover whatever it was that they wanted to keep secret. *What could that be?* she wondered as she finished cleaning the mirror.

Sitting on the edge of the bed trying to clean her foot, Donnie couldn't get the warning out of her mind. Maybe she should share all of these strange events with someone, but with whom?

Rodney was stubborn as a mule and rude to the point that she didn't care if she ever saw him again. Besides, she wasn't all that sure that he wasn't behind some of her accidents.

Julie wasn't speaking to her, and she didn't really want to

tell her grandmother.

Terry, maybe, but she needed to know the handsome father of Mark a little better before she could even trust him.

Slipping on a pair of yellow shorts and a yellow and white top, Donnie decided to keep quiet at least for now about her latest ordeal.

Heading down the hallway she couldn't help wondering once more if she could trust any of the strange people that she had met since coming to the inn. Hurrying to a large patio that was attached at the back of the inn, Donnie found Mark sitting playing with a set of cars as he waited for her. First, she had him read to her, which he did quite well.

Then, she gave him a math test. Here she found that he needed to improve. They spent the next hour working on addition.

"You two look like you need a break," said Terry as he approached them carrying a basket and a red and white blanket. "I had Granny Kelly pack us some of her special Cedar Key pie and thought the three of us might head for the beach to share it."

With a pleading look from Mark, Donnie knew it was about time to stop for the day. "I guess we could use a little R and R," said Donnie. "I just hope you haven't planned on going to far," she said as she pointed to the now bandaged foot.

"Don't worry about walking," said Terry as he led Donnie and Mark to the end of the patio.

Parked on the sand below was a red and white dune buggy just waiting to take them wherever they wanted to go. Helping Donnie down from the patio, Terry reached over and gently picked her up. Handing the basket and blanket to the close following Mark, the trio headed down the beach to the buggy.

"Still helpless, I see," said Rodney with his usual harshness,

causing Terry to almost drop Donnie into her seat. "What's happened to you now that you need to be carried like some helpless child?" asked Rodney as he stood staring at this woman who seemed to always make him angry.

"We're going on a picnic," said Terry as he helped Mark put the basket and blanket in beside Donnie.

Donnie just sat and stared at Rodney with her heart pounding in her ears, not saying a word and turning her back on him as he started to speak again.

Why does this rude man make my heart beat so fast? thought Donnie as she continued to try and not look at him.

As Terry started the dune buggy, Donnie turned to see Rodney walking back down the beach.

"Where to, my lady?" asked Terry as they started down the beach.

"I don't really care, as long as that awful Rodney isn't there," said Donnie as Terry started off.

As they rode down toward the ocean, Donnie tried not to think about the way that Rodney always seemed to get under her skin. She was with Terry now, and she was going to enjoy herself if it killed her. She wasn't going to let Rodney spoil an afternoon of fun with Terry and Mark.

First, they stopped for a while and just looked out over the ocean. Mark got out and played for a while in the sand, while she and Terry sat and watched the tide as it came in and out.

"You're sure quiet," said Terry as they sat and watched Mark playing.

"Oh, I was just watching Mark playing and thinking how lucky you are to have each other," said Donnie, not wanting to tell Terry that she was deep in thought again over the things that had been happening to her.

"Mark, come on," yelled Terry. "I want to take you to our

special place to have our pie," he said as Mark jumped in the back of the dune buggy. "Mark's mom and I used to go to this spot a lot, and Mark just loves it," said Terry as a look of sadness came over him. "He doesn't remember her much, and this place is where he can be close to her," said Mark as he headed up the beach.

Suddenly Donnie saw where they were going. They were heading right for the bridge that she had crossed only hours before to enter the cove with the lighthouse. *The lighthouse and that crazy old man*, she thought as her mind raced back to the events that had taken place earlier that morning.

Why was Terry taking her there? Was he telling her the truth about taking her and Mark to his dead wife's special place, or was he part of what the old man was hiding? Was he the person that pushed her down the stairs last night? He was there when the lights came on. Why was he really taking her to the lighthouse? She wanted to scream.

"Stop, stop," were the words that Donnie wanted to shout, but before she could utter a sound, Terry stopped the buggy and jumped out, shouting something about Rodney.

At first Donnie didn't see where Terry was running to, but before she could ask anything, she heard the loud shouting coming from just inside the rocks that led to the cove.

Who's yelling? she wondered as she saw Terry disappear through the rocks.

"Stay here," shouted Donnie to Mark as she too jumped from her seat and started running toward the shouting....

Chapter 7

As Donnie neared the entrance to the rocks, she could now see two men pushing and yelling at each other. As she came closer, she soon realized that the two men fighting were Rodney and Hank, the old man from the lighthouse.

They were pushing and shoving, and saying something that Donnie couldn't hear.

Both men looked like two wild animals as they continued to yell. Rodney was doing most of the yelling as Hank tried to run.

Terry was now inside the rocks yelling for them to stop. Looking up from their argument, Rodney and Hank suddenly realized that they were no longer alone.

Noticing now that their uninvited guests had distracted Rodney, Hank pushed him to the ground and darted away heading back through the rocks, leaving him to answer questions about the fight that was taking place.

"Rodney, are you alright?" yelled Terry as he ran up beside him.

But before Rodney could answer him, Donnie ran through the rocks shouting, "Are you alright? Are you alright?" as she kneeled over the now battered Rodney.

"I'm fine," he shouted as he tried to push her hands away from his face as it began to sting.

"I'm fine. I don't need your help."

"Well, isn't this a little different?" said Donnie as she realized that for once it was Rodney on the ground and not her.

"What do you mean different?" yelled Rodney as he felt his heart racing as his face turned a bright red.

"You're on the ground for a change, instead of me," said Donnie just a little too smugly.

"Will you two stop your jabs?" came the sharp reply from behind them, causing Donnie and Rodney both to stop.

"What was going on, Rodney, between you and old man Hank?" asked Terry as he stood looking at the now red-faced pair.

"Nothing, nothing," said Rodney.

"NOTHING!" shouted Donnie as she once again reached out to touch the now bruising cheek of Rodney.

"I said nothing, and I mean NOTHING," yelled Rodney as he pulled away from Donnie and pulled himself up from the ground, heading toward the cove as Donnie and Terry stood watching.

"See what I'm telling you," said Donnie as she managed to speak as Rodney disappeared around the bend to the cove.

"Well, if you ask me, you two seem to enjoy all these arguments too much," said Terry as he turned and headed back toward the dune buggy.

"Enjoy? Enjoy? What are you talking about?" asked Donnie as she looked up from where Rodney had been only seconds ago.

"Never mind. Let's just get back to Mark and head for the inn. Our plans are ruined for today anyway," said Terry as he started up the sand toward Mark.

As Donnie started to follow, she suddenly felt a pain in her foot—a pain that she had forgotten all about.

Maybe Terry was right. Maybe she and Rodney did enjoy fighting. *Oh, don't be silly,* she thought as she limped her way back to Terry and Mark.

On the ride back to the inn, not a word was spoken between the once happy trio. Mark had fallen asleep in the back, and Donnie was pretending to look at the ocean as they drove along the beach, not wanting to start up again about Rodney.

Arriving at the steps of the inn, Donnie, forgetting her injured foot, jumped quickly from the dune buggy, hoping to escape without any more questions about her and Rodney.

Falling as she jumped out, tears now seemed to fill her eyes as the pain throbbed in her foot. Before she could even try to limp off, Terry was beside her, scooping her up in his arms and carrying her up the stairs of the inn.

Placing her in a large wicker chair, without a word, Terry just hurried back down the stairs and drove off into the almost darkness.

I think all the men on this island are nuts, thought Donnie as she watched the lights soon disappear towards the back of the inn.

"Well, there you are," said Granny Kelly as Donnie suddenly looked up. "I was starting to wonder if something else had happened to you, since I hadn't seen you all day."

"Oh, I went on a picnic with Mark and Terry," said Donnie, not wanting to tell her grandmother about the fight in the cove. "I'm sorry that I didn't tell you," said Donnie as she started to rise, once again forgetting about her sore foot.

"Let me help you into the kitchen," said Granny Kelly as she put her arm around Donnie's shoulder, and they headed for the door of the inn.

"I bet it's been awhile since you've eaten," she said as they stepped inside.

Hungry? thought Donnie. She was starved. In all of the excitement, she hadn't eaten at all.

"Yes, I am hungry, Granny," said Donnie as she sat down in

an almost empty dining room. Only a few guests remained, chatting over a last cup of coffee.

What a day, she thought as she waited for Granny Kelly to return from the kitchen.

"First, the fight and then Terry accusing her and Rodney of enjoying the fights that they always seemed to be having. Maybe he was right. Maybe we did enjoy them too much. Oh, how silly," Donnie mumbled.

"What was that you were saying?" asked Granny Kelly as she entered from the kitchen carrying a tray with something that smelled really good. "I don't have a lot left over, but at least this should keep you until breakfast," she said as she put the tray down on the table in front of Donnie.

"Oh, nothing," said Donnie as Granny began to set the leftovers from the evening meal in front of her.

There was a plate filled with homemade chicken and dumplings, a small salad, and homemade rolls that Granny Kelly had made earlier in the day. There was also a small piece of the inn's famous apple pie.

Without saying another word, Donnie began to eat like someone that hadn't eaten in days.

"Slow down, girl," said Granny Kelly as she watched Donnie almost swallowing the meal without taking a breath. "You act like you haven't eaten for days. Here, take a drink of water before you choke yourself," said Granny as she poured Donnie some water.

Donnie didn't even look up. She just kept eating, acting like someone might take her food away before she had eaten the last bite.

Finishing the last bite of the apple pie, Donnie let out a sigh that let Granny Kelly know that she was done. "Thanks so much Granny," said Donnie as she pulled herself up and tried to put

some weight on her now swollen foot.

"Here, let me help you," said Granny as she reached out for Donnie.

"No, I can make it myself," said Donnie as she pulled away from Granny Kelly. "I will take my time, and in no time I will be up those stairs sitting in a hot tub soaking my wounds, " she said as she limped off.

Slowly making her way up the stair of the inn, Donnie began to get that strange feeling in her stomach—a feeling that she seemed to be getting a lot since her arrival on Cedar Key Island.

"Oh, please let this silly feeling go away," said Donnie as she remembered all the strange things that had been going on.

Reaching her room, Donnie stood and just stared at the closed door. A sudden chill seemed to raise the hair on the back of her neck as she reached for the doorknob.

Is that a noise coming from inside my room, or is it coming from down the hall? Donnie thought as she slowly turned the knob.

"Oh, don't be foolish," she said as she pushed open the door and stepped inside a totally dark room.

Reaching now for the light switch, Donnie suddenly froze as she realized that she was not alone. Standing right in front of her was the black figure from the day before, staring at her with those same blue eyes that seemed to see right through her now—eyes that seemed to have her frozen to the very spot where she now stood.

Still unable to move, Donnie tried to scream, but before she could utter a sound, the black figure moved. It moved so quickly that Donnie could only hear the door as it slammed shut. In another second, the figure was pulling on her.

"Move, move," came the demanding voice, and all she could do was obey.

In another second, a door was opened, and Donnie was shoved inside yet another dark room. Falling now as the figure pushed harder, Donnie didn't even have a second to catch her breath as she heard the door slam and lock behind her….

Chapter 8

"Go home," came a muffled voice from the other side of the now locked door. "Go home!" Then nothing, not a sound came from the other side of the door.

Donnie just lay in the darkness, not moving, for fear that the figure in black would return to harm her.

Who is this person in black that keeps showing up, trying to scare me into going home? thought Donnie as she lay in the darkness.

Would he come back soon, and if he did, what would become of her?

Sitting up suddenly, Donnie realized that she must escape before the figure in black returned. *But how?* she wondered as she tried to feel something near her.

"What kind of a room have I been thrown into?" she said out loud as she once again tried to feel around her.

She soon found that the floor was covered with carpet and that there wasn't much room to move. Standing now as quietly as she could, Donnie began to try and touch anything that was near her in the darkness. If there was another way out, she didn't want the mysterious man in black to hear her fumbling around and come back.

Reaching in front of her now, Donnie suddenly stopped and realized where she was standing. She was standing in the middle of her closet. "It's my closet," Donnie whispered as she began to feel the clothes that hung near her.

Sitting down with a thud, Donnie knew now that the only

way out was the locked door that stood in front of her. As Donnie sat in the darkness, she was starting to wonder why she had ever come to Cedar Key Island. Then she heard it. The door of her room was opening, and someone was crossing toward her closet.

Should I cry out? she thought as her heart pounded harder inside her chest with each breath that she took. *What if it's the man in black?* she thought as she stood trying to now hide behind her clothes. *Has he come back to make sure that I leave forever?* she thought as she pressed her back against the wall of her closet.

Then the funniest thing happened. The wall behind Donnie seemed to just disappear, and before she could do anything, Donnie fell right through the back of her closet. She couldn't see a thing as she hit the floor, hitting her elbow as she went down.

Where am I? Donnie thought as she rubbed her now throbbing elbow.

It was so dark that she couldn't see a thing. Then she heard it. *Is that the key turning in the lock?* she thought as she tried to stand.

Is the mysterious man in black back to make sure that I leave or even worse? she said as she tried once again to see something in the darkness.

Standing up now, Donnie pressed her back up against what she assumed was the wall of the secret room that she had fallen into. Holding her breath, her heart was pounding so hard that she was sure that the man in black would hear it. Closing her eyes she waited for whatever was going to happen as she once again wished that she had never come to Cedar Key Island.

* * * * *

Donnie wasn't sure how long she stood waiting for her fate before she opened her eyes.

Is the man in black playing games with me? she thought as she took another deep breath. *Why hasn't he entered the closet and the hidden room?* she thought, while daring not to move.

In a few more minutes, she decided to move. At first, she took only a small step forward. Then, she stepped carefully inside the still dark closet.

"Maybe I didn't hear the key turn after all," she said softly as she stood very quiet just inside the closet.

Moving toward the door, Donnie put her ear against the door, hoping to hear the slightest sound from the other side. Nothing, not a sound could be heard. Reaching for the knob slowly, Donnie took another deep breath as she slowly turned it.

"Should I push it open?" she whispered as she took yet another deep breath and again tried to listen for the sound of someone breathing inside her room, but she could hear nothing.

"One, two, three," Donnie counted as she closed her eyes and slowly pushed the door open.

Slowly opening her eyes, Donnie stepped through the closet door into her bedroom. Looking around quickly, she soon found that she was alone.

The man in black was not waiting for her.

Then she heard someone moving in the hallway.

Maybe if I hurry, I can finally see the mysterious man in black, she thought as she moved quickly across the room.

Opening the door only a crack, Donnie's eyes took a moment to adjust to the sudden brightness of the hall light. At first she saw nothing, and then as her eyes began to focus, Donnie saw someone moving near the stairs.

Opening the door a little wider, she carefully put her head through the open door, and that's when she saw him!

Rodney Atwater was moving very slowly down the hall toward the stairs leading to the lobby below.

He wasn't just walking. He was almost creeping, looking from side to side as if he wanted to be sure that no one could hear him.

What is he doing? thought Donnie as she watched him reach the top of the stairs.

Suddenly realizing that Rodney was turning around, Donnie pulled her head back inside, hoping that he hadn't spotted her peeking out.

Once again holding her breath, Donnie's heart pounded. It was pounding so hard now that she was sure that Rodney would hear it. Moving once again toward the doorway, Donnie slowly peeked out again.

Rodney was gone.

Why had he been sneaking down the hall? thought Donnie as she moved back into the dark room, closing the door behind her.

"Why is he always around when trouble is near?" she asked herself as she turned on the light. "And why does he always make my heart pound when he is near," she said out loud. *Is it fear or something else?* she thought as she crossed to the open closet door.

"Donnie, are you up?" came the voice of Granny Kelly as Donnie jerked around. "What's wrong?" asked Granny Kelly as she crossed the room toward Donnie. "You're white as a sheet," she said as she stood in front of Donnie.

"Nothing," said Donnie, moving away from the closet door.

"Well, let's get some sun in here," Granny said as she pulled open the drapes.

Sun, thought Donnie, wondering how long she had been in that closet as she turned around noticing that Granny Kelly

was staring at her. “Why are you staring?” asked Donnie.

“Well, you look like you haven’t slept at all, and if you did sleep, you slept in your clothes.”

“Oh, I was so tired that I collapsed on the bed,” said Donnie as she decided not to tell Granny Kelly about spending the night locked in her closet. “Now, get out of here so I can take a shower and get yesterday’s clothes off,” said Donnie, taking Granny by the arm as she walked her toward the door. “You have people to feed,” said Donnie as she pushed Granny Kelly out the door and shut it quickly.

Crossing to the closet door, Donnie closed the door, deciding to wait until later to explore the hidden room....

Chapter 9

As Donnie stepped out of the shower, she couldn't get the secret room out of her mind. So many unanswered questions kept popping up in her head as she stood in front of the mirror.

How long had the room been there? she thought as she dried her hair. *Does the mysterious man in black know about the secret room?* she wondered as she opened the closet. *Maybe that's how he's getting in and out of my room,* she thought as she stepped inside.

"One thing for sure, if I don't find out about this secret room soon, I am going to bust," she said as she picked out a pair of blue shorts and a white tee shirt to wear for the day.

Then Donnie just stood staring at the back of her closet. *Maybe if I just take a peek*, she thought as she stepped closer to the entrance.

Peering now into the darkness, Donnie moved forward and then stopped as she heard the door of her bedroom opening.

"Donnie, where are you?" came the familiar voice of Julie.

"In here," yelled Donnie, stepping back from the dark entrance of the secret room.

"What are you doing?" Julie asked crossing the room toward the open closet door.

"Come in here," yelled Donnie, deciding that it was time to share the secret room with someone else.

"What are you doing in here?" Julie asked as she stepped inside.

"I have something that I want to show you," Donnie said as

she moved to the back of the closet.

"Where are you?" Julie asked, as Donnie seemed to disappear.

"I'm in here," Donnie said as her voice came from out of the darkness.

"Where are you?" said Julie as she carefully stepped through the entrance at the back of the closet.

"Right here," said Donnie in the darkness as she put a hand on Julie's arm, making her jump.

"I can't see a thing," said Julie as she tried to feel around in the darkness,

"Where are we?" she asked as she tried to see something in the darkness.

"It's some kind of secret room that I discovered last night when I was locked in my closet," said Donnie.

"Locked in your closet," said a now confused Julie.

"Come on. Let's go back into my room, and I will tell you everything," said Donnie as she pulled Julie back into her closet.

Donnie then spent the next thirty minutes telling Julie about all the mysterious things that had been happening to her since her arrival a few days before. When she was done, all Julie could do was stare at her.

"You're the only person that knows any of this," said Donnie as she finished dressing.

"Why would anyone want to harm you?" asked Julie as she shook her head.

"I really don't know," said Donnie.

"I know we need to find out more about the secret room," said Donnie as she crossed toward the closet again. "But not now," she said as she closed the closet door.

"Why not now?" asked Julie. "I want to see what's inside of that room. Don't you?"

"Not now," Donnie said again as she headed toward her bedroom door. "We need a plan. We need to eat breakfast and make a plan," she said as she stood in the open bedroom doorway. "Not a word about any of this. Not one word," Donnie said as she and Julie headed toward the stairs. "This is our secret," she said as they started down the stairs....

Chapter 10

As Donnie and Julie entered the inn's dining room from the lobby, they both noticed that Doc Phillips was sitting reading a paper as he drank his morning coffee.

"How is your foot, Donnie?" he asked as the girls neared him.

"Fine," answered Donnie as the two girls rushed past, leaving Doc Phillips to look at their backs as they entered the kitchen door.

"It's about time you two decided to show up," came the gruff voice of Granny Kelly.

"Sorry," said Donnie. "Julie and I were talking, and we just lost track of time," she said as she looked to see what might be left to eat from breakfast.

"There isn't much," said Granny Kelly as she pointed to a plate of the inn's famous cinnamon rolls. "Help yourself to some coffee too," Granny said as she headed out the door toward the dining room.

"Good," said Donnie as she poured a cup of coffee for her and Julie. "With Granny out of here, we can make our plans for the secret room," she said to Julie.

"I still can't believe that the inn has a secret room," said Julie as she placed two of the cinnamon rolls on plates for her and Donnie.

"Well, believe it or not, we both know there is one," said Donnie. "You're from Cedar Key, aren't you?" asked Donnie.

"Yes," said Julie.

"You've never heard anything about the inn having a secret room?" asked Donnie.

"Not a word," Julie answered as she got another cup of coffee. "I do know that the inn was a store and a post office in the 1800s, but I never heard anything about a secret room. I also know that during the Civil War, the town was occupied by the Union Army, and they used the inn as a barracks and a warehouse."

"Maybe the room was a place to hide from the enemy," said Donnie as she listened to Julie.

"Maybe it was used to hide slaves that were escaping," said Julie as she tried to picture someone hiding in the secret room, as people looked for them.

"I wonder if the local museum would have any information on the inn," said Donnie as she stood.

"Maybe it would have something on the secret room," said Julie as she stood also.

"Where are you two going?" asked Granny Kelly as she entered the kitchen carrying a tray loaded with dishes from the dining room left from breakfast.

"I am going up to start cleaning the rooms before you fire me," laughed Julie as she headed over to a small closet at the end of the kitchen to get the cart that she used each day to clean the inn's rooms.

"I need to find Mark and do a little work on his math," lied Donnie, not wanting to tell Granny Kelly where she was really going.

Once the two girls were out of the kitchen and in the lobby, they started once again to talk about the secret room.

"How far is the museum from here?" asked Donnie as she looked around the lobby, making sure that they were alone.

"It's not too far at all," said Julie as she headed over to a

map on the lobby wall. "Here we are, and here is where the museum is located," said Julie, pointing to the inn and the museum on the map.

"What time will you finish with the rooms?" asked Donnie as she looked at the map.

"It takes until lunch to get most of them cleaned," said Julie.

"So if I go to the museum now, you should be able to meet me for lunch," asked Donnie. "That way I can tell you what I find out and then we can make our plans to check out the secret room tonight," Donnie said as she headed for the inn's front doors.

Going down the stairs of the inn's porch, Donnie headed up the main street of Cedar Key Island. People seemed to be everywhere enjoying the shop filled streets. She noticed that not a lot had changed in the five years since her last visit.

Passing the many art galleries filled with painting from the many artists that seemed to fill the island each summer, Donnie knew why she loved this place. Only about a 1,000 people lived on the island, but it always seemed to be filled with tourists that were there to fish or just enjoy the sun as it rose and set each day.

It was said that watching the sun come up or go down was a thrilling event that even the island people enjoyed each day and made them never want to leave. Even in the winter it was always around 80 degrees and was the ideal place to fish, hike or just lie on the beach and watch the birds fly overhead.

Donnie just wished that all the strange things would stop happening to her, and now she had this secret room to find out about. All of these mysterious things were ruining her time here, and she resented that someone was trying to run her away from a place that she loved.

Rounding the corner, Donnie could see the St. Claire

Whitman house that was used as the island museum. It was an old house that reminded her of something that you would have seen in the South in the years of the Civil War.

It was almost as if you might expect to see a Southern belle sitting on the front porch, sipping a mint julep and fanning herself with a fancy lace fan.

Suddenly Donnie got that old feeling in the pit of her stomach as she climbed the stairs of the Whitman house—a feeling that she always hated to get these days. Turning around, Donnie noticed a man standing across the street that seemed to be staring at her.

Shading her eyes from the bright sun, Donnie tried to see who it was, but as she turned, the man suddenly turned and hurried back down the street.

"Maybe I am just too jumpy," Donnie said as she watched the man disappear around the corner from where she had just come.

Climbing the stairs, Donnie opened a door and stepped into the main hall of the museum. Like the outside of the house, the hallway reminded Donnie of a Southern home in the 1800s.

Walking over to the bottom of a spiral staircase, Donnie began to look for someone who could help her. Seeing a small desk to the right of the stairs, Donnie noticed a sign that said, "Ring the bell if I am not here at my desk."

Reaching down and tapping the bell twice, Donnie started to move toward the stairs when a woman came rushing in from a room near the back of the main floor. She was dressed in what Donnie thought looked like what a Southern woman had worn when the house was new.

"Can I help you?" asked the woman as she stepped behind the desk.

"Yes," said Donnie as she moved back toward the desk. "I

am looking for some information on the Jamaican Inn."

"What kind of information?" asked the woman.

"How was it built? Who has owned it over the years? And maybe how it survived the Civil War and so many hurricanes?"

"Follow me," said the woman as she headed toward the spiral staircase. "We have a room full of records on the second floor about many things on Cedar Key Island, and I am sure we can find something about the Jamaican Inn," she said as Donnie followed her up the stairs. "I can tell you several things myself about the inn. It's been owned by many people over time, and it wasn't always a hotel," the woman said as she pulled out a set of keys and opened a door at the far end of the hall.

Entering the room behind the woman, Donnie was surprised to see that the room was filled with box after box of records.

Watching the woman as she moved to the far end of the room, Donnie was starting to wonder if this was too big a job for just one person. She was starting to wish that Julie were there to help her.

Watching as the woman opened the drapes, Donnie hoped that somewhere in those boxes she would find the answer to the secret room, and why someone wanted her to leave Cedar Key Island....

Chapter 11

For the next several hours, Donnie poured over box after box trying to find even a word about the inn.

Maybe there isn't anything, she thought as she pulled another box out to go through.

"Maybe nothing was kept on the inn," she said as she sat the box on a table where she had been working all morning.

Looking at her watch, Donnie realized that it was almost lunchtime and she had told Julie that she would be back by lunch to make plans for the secret room.

Reaching for her cell phone, Donnie dialed the inn's number, hoping to reach Julie without Granny Kelly asking too many questions.

"Jamaican Inn," came the voice of Molly Hanks, the woman who answered the phone during the summer.

"Molly, this is Donnie. Can I speak to Julie?" she asked. "She is waiting for me in the dining room for lunch," said Donnie, hoping that her Granny wasn't anywhere around.

"Hello," said Julie.

"It's Donnie. I am still here at the museum, and I can't get back for lunch," she said. "Can you come and help me?" asked Donnie as she told Julie about all the boxes that she still needed to go through.

"No, I am helping Granny Kelly this afternoon to clean the porches," said Julie.

"Well, don't ask her if you can come. We don't want her to ask any questions," said Donnie. "I'll just stay here and keep

looking. I know there has to be something in one of these boxes," she said as she looked around her again. "I'll just plan to meet you after supper in my room," said Donnie. "Just don't say a word to Granny Kelly about any of this," said Donnie as she hung up.

"Can I get you anything?" asked the woman from downstairs as she entered the room.

"No, I just need to keep digging through these boxes," Donnie said as she opened yet another box.

"We close at 5:00," the woman said as she left.

Putting the box back, Donnie suddenly spied a large box almost hidden from sight behind several other boxes. Moving several boxes, Donnie pulled the large box to the front.

Opening it, Donnie began to read the papers she pulled from inside. As she read page after page about the early days of Cedar Key Island, she suddenly realized that she was starting to read about the inn.

> In the early 1800s Cedar Key Island was a seaport and had the first railroad going to the East Coast. Somewhere between 1859-1860, a building was built at the far end of town. The walls were made from mixed oyster shell, limestone and sand. They were 10 inches thick when they were done. This building was built to survive the many hurricanes, floods and storms that are a part of the everyday life on Cedar Key Island.
>
> This building was first used as a store and a post office. When the Civil War came, the Union army burned most of the town, but kept the building to use as a barracks and a warehouse. After the war, the next owner used it as a boarding house and sold meals.
>
> In 1896, a hurricane struck and destroyed much of

> the town again, but the building survived again. For several years it sat idle. Once again in 1950 the building was almost destroyed by a hurricane that lasted for 17 hours, and again it survived.
>
> In 1973, after passing through many hands, a woman named Mary Kelly bought the building, and it was then renamed the Jamaican Inn.
>
> Mrs. Kelly did many repairs to the inn, including putting a new restaurant where an old bar had been for many years. She set very high standards for the restaurant and made many of the dishes that the restaurant has become famous for.
>
> Mrs. Kelly still owns the inn and has received many good reviews on the inn as well as it famous restaurant.

Reading a few pages more, Donnie soon found that there didn't seem to be any more mentioned about the inn.

Not a word about a secret room, she thought as she put the papers back in the box. "So when had the room been built, and who built it?" she asked herself as she turned to close the drapes behind her.

Looking out before she closed them, Donnie saw that the once bright sky seemed to have clouded over while she had been busy searching for an answer to even one of the many questions that were spinning around in her head.

In fact, it looked like a storm might be coming and soon.

Turning out the lights as she hurried out into the hall, Donnie suddenly realized just how dark the hallway had become since she first entered the records' room several hours before.

Hurrying as fast as she could, Donnie suddenly felt that she wasn't alone. Looking from side to side as she almost ran to the top of the stairs, Donnie ran down into the lobby.

Looking back up the staircase into the dark hallway, Donnie could almost feel the eyes of someone as they stood in the shadows at the top of the stairs.

Maybe the man in black stood watching, thought Donnie as she tried to see into the dark hallway.

Not a sound could be heard as Donnie made her way over to the desk by the staircase. Seeing that the woman in charge wasn't anywhere around, Donnie rang the bell once again.

The woman came out at once and was now dressed in a pair of jeans with a pink and white top.

"I thought I was going to have to come up and get you," said the woman as she stepped from behind the desk. "Did you find what you needed?" she asked as she started toward the front doors of the museum.

"I found a little about the inn, but not a lot," said Donnie not moving.

"Well, it's after 5:00, and the museum is closed," said the woman standing by the doors. "Besides, a storm is coming, and I want to get out of here before it comes," she said rather rudely to Donnie.

"Are we alone here?" asked Donnie still not moving.

"We are now," said the woman. "There was a man here earlier that just wanted to see the museum," she said as she opened the door.

"Did you know him?" asked Donnie.

"Yes, it was that Rodney Atwater," said the woman as Donnie stared at her when she heard the name.

"Did you see him leave?" asked Donnie as she looked up the stairs again into the darkness.

"No, but I was in the back reading," said the woman. "Now, I need for you to leave," came the gruff voice of the woman as she pointed toward the door. "From the looks of the sky, you

had better hurry wherever you're going or you might get caught in a storm, and storms are something you don't want to be out in around here," said the woman as she all but pushed Donnie out the door.

Stepping out on the porch, Donnie couldn't get Rodney out of her mind. *Why had he been at the museum?* she thought as she went down the steps of the museum. *Is he following me?* she wondered as she crossed the street looking behind her at the house she had just left. *Is Rodney helping the man in black? If not, why is he always around when things happen to me?* she thought to herself as she stared at the dark windows of the museum.

Taking one last look at the dark windows, Donnie stopped moving and just stared at the window of the room she had been in earlier.

Was she seeing things in the dark, or was that a light she saw moving behind the closed drapes? Maybe the woman who worked there had gone back up to make sure that she…

Then the strangest feeling came over Donnie as she stared at that dark window—a feeling that she was being watched at from the darkness of the upstairs window. *Is Rodney there in the darkness staring at me? Had he left earlier, or is he still there hidden in the darkness, waiting for me and the other woman to leave?*

Maybe I am seeing things, Donnie thought as she decided to head for the inn before the storm hit.

Turning her back on the dark window, Donnie began to make her way up the lighted streets of Cedar Key, feeling that she had missed something big in the museum, but just not sure what.

Inside the dark room, a figure in black watched as she rounded the corner and out of sight, before he turned on the small light that Donnie had seen only moments before….

Chapter 12

As Donnie neared the inn, the wind seemed to be picking up. Hurrying up the front steps of the inn, Donnie barely had time to step inside the lobby of the inn before a strong gust pulled the door right out of her hands, slamming it loudly against the front wall of the inn with a loud bang.

"Here, let me help you," said Rodney as he grabbed the still moving door, pushing Donnie out of the way as he tried to hold on to the door.

Falling backwards, Donnie landed on the floor with a loud thud, and all she could do was sit there with her heart thumping strangely as she watched Rodney struggling as he pushed the door shut.

"What's all the noise in here?" said Terry as he entered the lobby from the inn's dining room, followed closely by Mark.

"Nothing," said Rodney as he crossed the room toward Donnie.

"You don't have to say another word," said Terry, seeing Donnie trying to get up from the floor before Rodney could get to her.

"Don't you two ever stop falling or knocking each other down?" asked Terry as he watched Donnie pushing Rodney's hands away as he tried to help her up.

"I can get up myself," shouted Donnie as she tried to push Rodney away. She didn't hear a word that Terry said.

"Is that so?" said Rodney as he stood over Donnie looking into those beautiful eyes, now filled with anger. "It seems to

me you're the person that came tearing into the inn trying to tear a hole in the side of the wall," said Rodney laughing.

"I DON'T NEED YOUR HELP," shouted Donnie as her heart thumped wildly as she stared up into Rodney's huge smile. "In fact, you're the reason I'm sitting down here," roared Donnie as she felt her face getting hotter and hotter from the anger she was feeling toward Rodney at that moment.

"Will you two stop your shouting?" said Granny Kelly as she too entered the lobby from the dining room. "I don't think my guests want to hear the two of you fighting while they are trying to enjoy their meal," she said as she moved toward Donnie.

"I know I am tired of listening to these two spoiled brats bickering all the time," said Terry as he and Mark turned and headed toward the stairs.

Donnie pulled herself up as Rodney, and Granny Kelly watched Terry and Mark disappear up the lobby stairs, standing she started moving slowly toward the doorway leading into the dinning room.

"I don't know about you two, but I am having my dinner," she said as Rodney and Granny Kelly turned in time to watch her disappear through the doorway.

Not looking back, Donnie hurried into the crowded dining room, hoping that Rodney wouldn't follow her. Looking for an empty table, Donnie spotted a table near a small set of windows, close to the kitchen door. Crossing the crowded room, Donnie spoke to several of the inn's guests as they looked up from their evening meals to speak when she passed them.

Sitting down at the small table, Donnie noticed how black the sky looked through the two bay windows that overlooked the yard at the side of the inn. Lightning appeared again and again in the dark sky as it lit up the two windows, making

Donnie jump as she reached for the menu.

Donnie looked up just as Granny Kelly entered the room minus Rodney. Donnie hoped she didn't see him the rest of the night.

"What can I get you, Miss Donnie," said Denise, the inn's longest working waitress, making Donnie jump again. "Sorry," she said as she stood watching Donnie, trying not to rush her as she looked at the menu. "I didn't mean to make your jump," she said as she waited.

"How about a bowl of clam chowder and a small plate of the shrimp," said Donnie as she decided that she wasn't too hungry after all.

Looking up from the menu after Denise left the table, Donnie noticed that Granny Kelly was making her way from table to table, trying to talk with many of the tourists that were staying at the inn. She was also talking to the local islanders that came to the inn for a taste of the famous seafood dishes that Granny Kelly was famous for creating over the years.

Once again Donnie looked out the windows as another flash of lightning lit up the dark sky and the yard below, and that's when she noticed something strange, something that made her sit straight up in her chair and not move as she stared out into the darkness. As another flash came, Donnie still didn't move. She just stared, waiting for another flash, wanting to make sure of what she was seeing.

Then another flash came and lit up the windows just enough for Donnie to see the dark figure that was standing right next to the bay windows, staring in at her.

The man in black whispered something as she stood up, leaning over to the window, trying to see into the darkness. As another flash came, Donnie looked again, but the figure was gone.

"What's wrong now?" asked Granny Kelly as she almost ran across the room, noticing Donnie standing with her face pressed up against one of the bay windows by her table.

Donnie didn't move. She just stared at the now empty window as it was lit up again by the lightning.

"I said what's wrong," said Granny as she put her hand on Donnie's arm, causing her to scream. "Come with me," said Granny as she pulled Donnie into the kitchen away from the staring diners. "I don't know what that was all about, but your foolishness is starting to affect my business," said Granny making Donnie sit down.

"It was nothing," said Donnie trying to stand.

"Then why did you jump up and scream when I touched your arm?" asked Granny.

"It was the lightning," Donnie said as she thought about the man in black staring back at her through the bay windows.

"Well, the look on your face doesn't say nothing," scolded Granny Kelly.

"Why does everyone around here make such a big deal of things?" asked Donnie as she tried to stand.

"Why do you act like a spoiled brat these days?" asked Granny.

"A spoiled brat. What do you mean by a spoiled brat?" asked Donnie.

"Yes, a spoiled brat," yelled Granny Kelly. Even Terry thinks you're a spoiled brat and so does Rodney Atwater."

"Rodney, Rodney Atwater."

"Who cares what Rodney Atwater thinks," yelled Donnie as her face glowed brightly.

"Well, I think you care what he thinks," said Granny.

"Well, I don't," yelled Donnie as she stood, almost knocking Granny Kelly down as she rushed out of the kitchen door.

"What's all the noise?" said Julie as Donnie stormed from the kitchen.

"Oh, nothing," said Donnie heading back toward the small table by the bay windows.

Moving to the table, Julie sat down noticing that Donnie seemed to be busy looking out into the darkness.

"What are you looking at?" asked Julie as another flash of lightning crossed the black sky.

"I am looking for the man in black," said Donnie, almost in a whisper.

"The man in black," whispered Julie as she too stared out into the dark night.

"Yes, the man in black," said Donnie as she looked to make sure that Granny Kelly had stayed in the kitchen. Turning from the windows, Donnie leaned across the candle lit table. "Not, ten minutes ago, I saw him standing right there," said Donnie as she pointed at the dark windows, causing Julie to once again look out into the darkness. "He was staring right at me."

"Do you think anyone else saw him?" asked Julie.

"I don't think so," said Donnie, her voice cracking as she spoke.

"Do you know what scares me the most? It scares me that he is getting braver. I can't believe that he would show himself with a room full of people, taking the chance that someone besides you might see him," said Julie as Denise came with Donnie's clam chowder.

"Do you want anything, Miss Julie?" asked Denise as she set Donnie's bowl of chowder down.

"Jut a cup of coffee will do," said Julie wanting Denise to leave so she could hear more about the man in black. "I can't understand why he is after you," said Julie

"Well, I sure don't know why he is after me either," said

Donnie.

"How did things go at the museum today? Julie asked, changing the subject. "Did you find anything about the secret room?"

"Not a thing," Donnie said as she tried to finish her chowder. "I only found out that the inn has survived many storms over the years and that different people have owned the inn in the last 200 years. I did find a part that told about how the Union Army took over the inn for years, but not a word about the secret room," she said. "I also had something strange happen to me while I was there," said Donnie, as Denise appeared with Donnie's plate of shrimp and Julie's coffee.

"What do you mean strange?" asked Julie after Denise had left the room.

"When I left the upstairs room of the museum, I felt as if I wasn't alone," said Donnie in a low voice. "I felt like someone was watching me. Then when I was leaving, the woman in charge of the museum told me something even stranger. She told me that Rodney Atwater had been at the museum this afternoon too."

"Rodney," whispered Julie with a surprised tone in her voice now.

"She wasn't even sure when he left or if he did leave," whispered Donnie, looking at the door leading out into the lobby, making sure that Rodney wasn't anywhere close enough to hear what she was saying. "In fact, he was just here," Donnie said as she turned staring out into the darkness.

"Here?" asked Julie.

"In the lobby, only a few minutes before the man in black appeared here outside this window," said Donnie. "I've told you before that it's really funny that he's always around when strange things happen to me."

Rising, Donnie motioned to Julie to follow her out into the lobby. Looking around to make sure that the lobby was empty, Donnie crossed the room with Julie following.

Leading Julie behind the lobby's check in desk, she opened a door behind the desk and stepped inside a large closet filled with extra towels, wash clothes, soap and other things needed to supply a room for the inn's guests.

Looking around inside the closet, Donnie soon found what she was looking for. There in the very back of the middle shelf lay two lights, shaped liked lanterns.

"Here, take this," she said as she handed one of the lights to Julie. "See if yours works," Donnie said as she pushed the on button of her light.

"What are you two doing in there?" asked Granny Kelly as she leaned over the lobby desk, trying to see what the two girls were doing.

"Oh, nothing," answered both girls, hiding the lights behind them.

"I was just checking to see if I needed to add anything to the closet before I go upstairs," lied Julie as she pushed her light under the lobby desk. "Everything is fine," she said as Donnie moved closer, placing her light under the desk beside hers.

"Have you settled down since you left the kitchen?" Granny Kelly asked Donnie.

"I'm fine now," she answered. "I'm sorry that I was acting so strange earlier," Donnie said trying to push the two lights further under the desk. "I think it was just all that awful lightning and all that goofy stuff with Rodney earlier that set me off," Donnie said, wishing she hadn't mentioned Rodney's name to Granny Kelly.

"Well, if you ask me, you're sure worried about Rodney Atwater a lot these days," said Granny Kelly with a smirk on

her face.

"Please, let's not start that again," said Donnie, wishing that Granny Kelly would leave, so the two girls could go search the secret room upstairs.

"All I know is that you and Rodney seem to spend a lot of time trying to convince me that you can't stand each other," said Granny as she turned and headed toward a door at the far end of the lobby that led into her apartment.

"Turn off the lights and lock the doors before you two go upstairs," she said to the two girls as she disappeared into her rooms.

"Is she gone?" asked Donnie as she reached for the two lanterns hidden under the desk. "Hurry and lock the door before she comes back."

Turning off the last light, the two girls took a deep breath as Donnie handed Julie one of the lights from behind the desk.

Moving slowly up the stairs and down the hallway toward Donnie's room, neither girl spoke a word. Both were deep in thought about the mysterious room and all the secrets that it held....

Chapter 13

Before entering Donnie's room, Julie looked back down the hallway, making sure that no one was watching them.

"What are you doing?" asked Donnie, turning on her bedroom light.

"Making sure that we aren't being followed," answered Julie as she looked out into the hall one more time.

Closing the door quietly, Julie crossed the room and sat down on the pink and white bed beside Donnie. "Ok, what's the plan," she asked Donnie.

"I'm not really sure if we have a plan. I just know that we need to find out what's in that room," said Donnie pointing toward her closet.

"Well, let's get to it then," said Julie as she stood and walked to the closet.

Jumping up, Donnie followed close behind.

Stepping inside the closet, Julie pulled the clothing aside so they could see the back of the closet wall where the entrance still stood open from the night before.

"Turn on your light," said Donnie as she switched on the light in her hand.

Shining it through the dark hole, Donnie stepped inside, followed by Julie.

Moving the lights from side to side, Donnie and Julie soon found that the room was empty. There wasn't anything on the brown wooden walls and nothing but dust on the floor beneath them.

"I can't believe there isn't anything here," said Julie as she kept shining the light from side to side. "We don't know anymore than you did last night when you sat in here in the dark," Julie said as she turned to leave the secret room.

"Wait!" shouted Donnie as she moved to the far end of the room, shining her light into the blackness.

Julie moved back inside the room, and when she did, she saw what Donnie was yelling about. At the far end of the room, the wall to the left of them was gone. Donnie stood shining her light through another opening, showing them a hidden tunnel that seemed to disappear into the blackness.

Looking at each other, Julie and Donnie stepped inside the dark tunnel. Shining the lights from side to side as they entered the tunnel, they soon decided that the tunnel had to be behind the closets of the rooms on Donnie's floor of the inn.

"Where are you going?" asked Julie as Donnie moved forward.

"I'm going to see where this leads," she answered as she disappeared into the darkness.

"Wait!" shouted Julie as she followed. "Are you sure that you want to keep going?" asked Julie as she almost ran over Donnie.

"Yes, I'm sure," said Donnie as she kept moving forward.

Donnie and Julie moved through tunnel after tunnel behind the walls of the inn, not saying a word, until suddenly the tunnel came to an end right in front of a huge wooden door.

Stepping forward, Donnie shined her light up and down the wooden door, wondering where this new entrance might lead them.

"Stop, don't open that," Julie said as she pulled Donnie away from the door.

"Why not open it?" asked Donnie moving back toward the closed door.

"What if it leads into someone's closet? What if it leads into the closet of the man in black," she asked as Donnie stopped. "Maybe that's how he gets from room to room so fast, without being seen," Julie said when Donnie didn't answer. "Or it might even lead to Granny Kelly's closet, and how would you explain being in her closet in the middle of the night?" asked Julie as she waited for Donnie to say something.

"I don't care whose closet it might be. I'm going to open this door right now," she said as she pulled on the latch before Julie could say another word.

The huge door swung open as the two girls looked inside. Holding her light in front of her, Donnie shined it right into yet another dark tunnel—a tunnel that seemed to be heading downhill, from what Donnie could see.

"Come on." She motioned to Julie with her light, as she stepped inside the new tunnel.

"Donnie, are you sure that you want to do this?" asked Julie as she reluctantly stepped inside herself.

"Close the door," said Donnie as she headed down the tunnel path again.

Quietly pulling the door shut, Julie followed, hoping that they knew what they were getting into.

Making their way downhill, tunnel after tunnel, Donnie and Julie felt a coldness that seemed to be seeping in through the walls as they trudged onward.

Shining their lights toward the ceiling above them, they found that the wood had now been replaced with dirt.

"I think we've left the Inn," said Donnie as they both stared up at the dirt ceiling, wondering where this tunnel was taking them.

"I don't really like this," said Julie as she was starting to wish that she were back in her warm bed at the inn.

Chapter 14

"I wish I had never let you talk me into coming into this horrible place," said Julie almost in tears, as she once again stood staring at a closed wooden door.

"I didn't talk you into anything," said Donnie as she suddenly turned to see a small light appear in the tunnel behind them. "In fact, you couldn't wait to see what was in the secret room behind my closet."

"That part is true, but I didn't want to go through that last door," said Julie. "You just stepped right through that door and took off, before I could say a word."

"Well, you didn't have to follow," Donnie said now in a rather sharp tone.

"What was I suppose to do, just stand there in the darkness alone?" asked Julie.

"It doesn't matter now whose idea it was to come this far because we are here standing in front of a locked door, and whoever is at the end of that light will be here soon too," said Donnie as she focused once again on the oncoming light, causing Julie to look too. "All that matters now is where are we going to hide when that light comes around that last bend," whispered Donnie. "Maybe if we move over this way, we can crouch down enough that the light won't shine directly on us. I don't think the person carrying the light is expecting anyone to be here, and if we're lucky, they will just shine the light on the door and not all around this tunnel," said Donnie moving closer toward the locked door.

Holding on to Julie, Donnie could feel her trembling as they prepared to crouch together in the corner by the door, not saying a word.

Why had I been so foolish to think that coming into this tunnel was a good idea? she thought. She wouldn't admit this to Julie, but she was sorry that she had dragged her into this newest danger—a danger that would soon round the corner, and all they could do was hope that they were hidden well enough to avoid being caught.

Crouching with their faces pressed to the wall of the tunnel, Donnie and Julie could smell the mold that seemed to be seeping up through the dirt floor beneath them.

Holding their breath as a light filled the tunnel, Donnie and Julie heard their hearts pounding in their ears as they covered their heads, waiting to be grabbed from behind, but nothing happened.

Moving her head just a little, Donnie could see two men standing not an inch from Julie's leg. They were so close that if Julie even flinched, she would touch them.

Why don't they see us? Donnie wondered as a cramp began to creep up her leg, as she watched the men leaning over something on the opposite wall.

"Here, hold this light while I get the key," said one of the men as he reached inside a small hole near the locked door.

Donnie watched as the man holding the light shined it on the huge padlock as the other man shoved a key into it.

A loud clicking sound could be heard as the padlock came open.

Stepping backwards even closer to the girls, the man with the light watched as the locked door swung open.

Watching as the man with the light moved around the door, Donnie and Julie were once again in total darkness. The girls

changed position as they realized that they were hidden behind the huge wooden door.

Listening as the two men talked on the other side of the door, Donnie and Julie tried to rub their now cramping legs.

"Put the key back," said one of the men. "That way it will be there if he wants to use it later tonight."

"I don't think he will come down here tonight, with that snoopy girl still running around," one of the men said, making Donnie listen even harder.

"If you ask me, he should just get rid of her before she finds out about the stuff in this room," answered the other man.

Still not moving, Donnie and Julie listened as the one man placed the key back into its secret hiding place.

"Willie, shine that light over here so I can switch the lights on in here," yelled one of the men.

Donnie and Julie looked at each other as the dark tunnel was illuminated with light. They were glad to be hidden behind the wooden door.

Moving around in their small hidden space, the girls discovered why the two men hadn't seen them earlier. Without knowing where they were in the darkness, the girls had crawled into a large opening, which hid them from sight.

"Close that door," yelled one of the men.

Watching as the huge wooden door was pulled shut, Donnie and Julie knew that it was time to move from the safety of their hidden space.

Shoving Julie through the large opening, Donnie rolled over quickly. Following into the darkness, Donnie suddenly stopped.

"The lights," Donnie whispered as she turned, moving back toward the hidden opening, almost falling as she groped around in the darkness.

Julie didn't stop. She just kept going feeling her way along

the wet dirt walls.

Entering the opening, Donnie soon found the lights. Picking them up, Donnie moved back out into the dark tunnel.

Turning to make sure that the door was still closed, Donnie turned on both lights as she started back through the tunnel.

Hurrying through tunnel after tunnel, Donnie was starting to wonder how far Julie had gotten in the darkness, when suddenly there right in front of her sat Julie rubbing her ankle.

"What happened?" asked Donnie as she neared Julie, shining a light on her.

"I turned around to see if you were still behind me, and I tripped on something in the dark," said Julie rubbing her ankle.

"I went back to get these," Donnie said as she looked closer at Julie's ankle. "Can you stand on it?" she asked.

"I don't know," answered Julie as she started to stand.

"Try putting some weight on it. Now, try and walk," said Donnie holding on to her left arm.

"It hurts," Julie moaned trying to take a step and not cry.

"I know it hurts, but you have two choices. You can stay here and wait for the men behind the door to come back this way, or you can hold on to me and limp back through these tunnels to my closet."

"I'll take my chances with you," answered Julie.

"Hand me one of those lights, and let's get out of here," she said, pulling one of the lights out of Donnie's hand.

With Donnie helping Julie through the maze of tunnels, the girls were soon back at the door that had led them into the second set of tunnels.

Opening the door, Donnie helped Julie step carefully through to the other side, before she pushed the door shut.

"We're almost there," Donnie said as they once again headed into the tunnels.

"I think I can make it without your help, now that we are off of that slick dirt. See, I can stand alone," she said as she headed down the tunnel on her own.

Quickly the two girls hurried through the last of the tunnels, entering the secret room at the back of Donnie's closet. Stepping back through the secret entrance, Donnie and Julie felt safe for the first time since they had left earlier that night.

"Not a word to anyone about this," Donnie said as she set her light down on the floor by her bed. "We don't know who we can to trust, and I don't want to scare Granny Kelly," she said as Julie started to protest.

"I still don't think it's a good idea to keep this a secret," said Julie.

"Well, then you tell me who we can trust," asked Donnie.

"I am not sure," Julie said.

"Then we aren't telling anyone," insisted Donnie.

"Alright, but I think it's a big mistake," said Julie. "Those men wanted you done away with, and if they find out about me, I am sure they will want the same for me."

"Well, before anyone can do away with either of us, I am going back in that tunnel tomorrow night to find out once and for all what's in that last door," said Donnie trying to act like the threat from the unseen men didn't bother her.

"Go back," Julie almost yelled.

"Yes, go back," answered Donnie. "You can come with me, or you can just stay in your bed with your head covered and never know what's hidden in that room," snapped Donnie.

"Alright, alright, I'll come back tomorrow night and help you," said Julie, knowing that she would be sorry.

"Remember not a word," said Donnie as Julie crossed to leave.

"Okay, but I still think we're making a huge mistake even

talking about going back," Julie answered. "I'll see you in the morning. We had better get some sleep, if we're going to run around in those dark tunnels again tomorrow night," said Julie as she stepped out into the hall, shutting Donnie's door.

Sitting on the edge of her bed alone now, Donnie couldn't get the secret room or the tunnels out of her mind.

Sleep? Who could sleep knowing that behind her closet stood a secret room leading to miles and miles of tunnels that led to another secret door—a door that she felt had all the answers as to why someone wanted her off Cedar Key Island....

Chapter 15

It took what seemed liked hours for Donnie to fall asleep. She couldn't get the secret room or the tunnels out of her mind. Once she had even gotten out of bed to put a chair against the closet door, fearing that the men from the tunnel might come into her room. When she finally did fall asleep, Donnie kept dreaming that she was running through the tunnels unable to find her way out.

Just before sunrise, Donnie gave up trying to sleep and got up.

Crossing her room, Donnie pulled open the drapes to reveal a spectacular view from her window as the sun was rising. She stood for a long time just enjoying the breathtaking view, not thinking once about the secret room or the maze of tunnels behind it.

Leaving the window, Donnie's thoughts returned to the events of the night before. Who were those men in the tunnel last night? What were they hiding in that locked room? Question after question kept spinning around in Donnie's head.

Dressing quickly, Donnie was soon on her way downstairs to see how Julie had survived the night.

She found her already eating by the same windows where Donnie had seen the man in black the night before. Donnie waved at Julie as she poured herself a cup of coffee from the large urn set up at the far end of the dining room for breakfast.

"How did you sleep last night?" asked Donnie as she sat down across from Julie.

"Not too good. Every time I closed my eyes, I felt like I was back in the darkness in one of those endless tunnels," said Julie as she took a bite out of her toast.

"I didn't sleep good either," said Donnie. "I don't know about you, but I have to know what's behind that locked door and soon," said Donnie, looking around making sure that no one was listening to what she was saying.

For all Donnie knew, anyone in the room could have been one of the men in that tunnel last night, and she didn't want to be overheard talking about it.

Looking out the window, Donnie noticed that the sunshine from earlier was covered with dark black clouds.

"Granny Kelly told me that a large storm front is just off the coast, and we may be in for a hurricane later today," said Julie as she too looked out the window.

Looking beyond the inn's yard, Donnie could already see the gigantic waves that were developing in the ocean below them.

"Have you ever been here through a hurricane?" Donnie asked Julie.

"Not here at the inn," answered Julie. "I was at my aunt Sue's house once when a very strong wind blew all the trees down at the bottom of Rogers' Hill, where she lived. I was only nine, and I thought for sure that I was going to be blown right into the ocean."

"I've never been here when one has hit, and I can say I am not looking forward to the idea that one may hit here tonight," said Donnie. "At least we know the inn has survived many storms before, so we should at least be safe here," she said as she stood. "I need to go tutor Mark, if Terry is still speaking to me after the snit he's been in over Rodney lately. Can you meet me in my room after supper tonight?" Donnie asked as Julie

rose also.

"I guess, but I am not sure that I want to follow you back through those tunnels to that locked room," said Julie.

"That's up to you, but I am going with or without you," Donnie said as she turned to leave the room.

Entering the lobby, Donnie found Mark sitting at one of the wicker tables near the front doors, alone.

Terry wasn't around, and that really suited Donnie. This way she could work with Mark and not have to hear about Rodney Atwater and all the other foolishness that Terry had been spouting about the two of them for the last few days.

Donnie and Mark worked most of the morning. First on math and then Mark read a few chapters of a book he had been reading to Donnie the last 15 or 20 minutes of their time together.

"I don't know about you, Mark, but I am ready for some lunch," said Donnie as Mark stopped reading.

"You go ahead. I want to finish this chapter and wait for my dad," said Mark picking up his book and starting to read, this time to himself.

Donnie was glad that she didn't have to see Terry, so she left Mark reading and went to find Granny Kelly to see what she had fixed for lunch.

The rest of the day went by very slowly, as Donnie tried to keep busy, while waiting to return to the secret room and the locked door. She didn't see much of Julie, but knew that more than likely she was busy cleaning the guestrooms of the inn.

Donnie even tried to sleep later in the afternoon, but the approaching storm kept getting worse as the wind picked up, banging the shutters against the side of the inn, right outside her bedroom windows.

Giving up, Donnie decided to go downstairs and help Granny

Kelly in the kitchen, but before she could get to there, Donnie bumped right into Rodney as he came in out of the storm.

"Sure is a mess out there," he said looking up and seeing Donnie.

Not answering, Donnie continued on her way to the kitchen to see Granny Kelly, trying to act like she hadn't heard Rodney and hoping that he wouldn't follow her. However, before she could say a word to Granny Kelly, in came Rodney following right behind her.

"What can I do for you two?" asked Granny Kelly as she stopped filling the pie shell in front of her.

Moving behind Granny Kelly, Donnie still didn't say a word, wondering why Rodney had followed her.

"I don't know about Donnie, but I'm here to secure the inn before the storm hits," answered Rodney. "The wind has really picked up since this morning, and I don't think it's going to get any better. I thought maybe Terry and Doc Phillips could help too," said Rodney

"I also need to see if any of the guests want to leave before they close the bridge, since it's the only way out of here," said Granny Kelly. "In fact, Donnie, you can go with them if you want," said Granny Kelly turning around to face Donnie.

"Why would I leave?" asked Donnie.

"You've never been here during a hurricane before, and I just thought you might be safer on the mainland," answered Granny Kelly.

"That might be a good idea," said Rodney. "I am not going anywhere. If both of you can stay, so can I," snapped Donnie.

"Suit yourself. I don't care if you go or stay. I don't have time to worry about you and your usual nonsense," answered Rodney.

Not wanting to stand there and argue, Donnie decided to

just leave the room before Granny Kelly or Rodney could say another word.

Without saying another word, she just turned and made her way across the kitchen, leaving Granny Kelly and Rodney alone to make their plans for the coming storm.

Chapter 16

Everyone at the inn had spent most of the afternoon preparing for the coming storm. Rodney, Terry and even Doc Phillips had been outside attaching the hurricane shutters, hoping to help block out the driving winds and heavy rains.

It had been an awful job trying to hold the shutters against the windows of the inn as they tried to snap each shutter into place, while the strong winds and rain pounded them.

One gust was so strong that it nearly blew Rodney and Terry off their ladders as Doc Phillips tried to hold on to the both of them.

Inside the inn, Granny Kelly, Donnie and Julie were busy helping the guests that wanted to leave for the mainland while it was still safe.

All three women knew that it was only a matter of time before the only bridge to the mainland was flooded by the approaching storm, leaving no way off the island.

Working as fast as she could, Donnie knew that the approaching hurricane was going to soon move on to land, and if that happened, the heavy rains, strong winds and high waves would damage buildings, trees and even cars that were in its path.

As the last guest checked out, Donnie and Julie followed Granny Kelly into the kitchen.

"We need to make sure that we have enough supplies to help us get through this storm," Granny Kelly said as she opened a large door at the end of the kitchen. I still think that you girls

should go to the mainland where it's safe."

"We aren't going anywhere," said both girls at once.

Handing both girls a hurricane supply list, Granny Kelly stepped inside a large room filled with supplies for the inn.

"Look at your list and make sure that you take these things with you when you go to bed tonight," said Granny Kelly.

Looking at the list the girls saw what they would need to survive the approaching hurricane: water, cans of food, a first aid kit, a battery-operated radio, a flashlight, batteries, matches and candles.

"I want each of you to have what's on that list, and when Rodney, Terry and Doc Phillips come inside, I want them to have the same. They will all be staying here for the night, and I want to make sure that everyone has what they need in case the hurricane hits."

Finding several small boxes near the door, Donnie and Julie began to fill them from the supply list. They spent the next hour not only filling a box for themselves, but also for Rodney, Terry, Doc Phillips and Granny Kelly.

When they set the last box on the table in the inn's kitchen, Donnie saw that Granny Kelly had been busy too. She had been cooking. On the large kitchen table were eggs, bacon, potatoes, a plate of biscuits and two large pots of steaming coffee.

"Donnie, go hurry those men along before this food gets cold," Granny said, getting plates and cups from the cupboard.

Pulling the door open, Donnie was almost overpowered by the strong wind that blew across the porch where she stood. It was raining so hard that at first she couldn't even look up. In another minute she was wet from head to foot.

Moving closer to the porch steps, Donnie tried once again to raise her head against the strong wind as more rain pelted her face. In another minute she was turning back toward the

kitchen door. There was no way she was going anywhere to get anyone.

With the wind and rain pushing her across the porch, Donnie opened the kitchen door and all but fell back inside. Dripping wet, she turned and shoved the door closed.

Turning around, Donnie came face-to-face with Rodney, Terry and Doc Phillips. In the short time she had been outside, they had entered the kitchen and were dripping wet too.

"Here, take these before all of you come down with pneumonia," said Julie and Granny Kelly handing a towel to each of them.

"I think we need more than a towel," laughed Rodney and Terry looking at the wet Donnie standing in front of them.

Looking down at herself, Donnie started to laugh too. A towel wouldn't dry anything on her or the men that stood dripping in front of her.

"Go change then. I will warm the food while your gone," said Granny Kelly.

It was nearly midnight before Rodney, Terry, Mark, Doc Phillips, Julie and Donnie left Granny Kelly for their rooms. They had spent nearly four hours eating and just talking about putting up the shutters and telling stories about past hurricanes.

Outside, the wind and rain raged, but inside everything seemed to be cozy as Donnie and Julie handed out the hurricane kits.

"Come to my room in awhile," whispered Donnie to Julie when they were alone.

"Don't tell me you're still planning to go into the tunnels tonight," whispered Julie.

"Just come to my room," said Donnie, leaving Julie alone in the kitchen.

Making sure that the kitchen door was locked, Julie picked

up her box of supplies and turned out the lights before heading to Donnie's room.

Julie could hear the wind as it beat against the side of the inn. Entering the hall leading to Donnie's room, Julie watched Rodney entering a room right across from Donnie's and Doc Phillips enter right next door.

At least everyone is close by, Julie thought, knocking on Donnie's door.

Opening the door, Donnie pulled Julie quickly inside.

"Did anyone see you come in here?" asked Donnie.

"I think Rodney and Doc Phillips both saw me. Rodney is across the hall, and Doc Phillips is right next door," answered Julie.

"I am not worried about Doc Phillips. It's Rodney that worries me," said Donnie.

"I think you're wrong about Rodney. I've known him for a long time, and I think you're wrong about him," said Julie.

"Think whatever you want, but I don't trust him. I don't like him being this close to us, and the tunnels," said Donnie sitting down on the bed.

"All you think about are those stupid tunnels and that locked door," said Julie.

"Well, if you think it's all so stupid, I'll just go by myself tonight," said Donnie heading for the closet.

"I can't believe you want us to go in there tonight with a hurricane about to hit."

"I think it's a great time to go."

Opening the closet door, Donnie disappeared inside, leaving Julie standing, wondering if she should follow.

Following Donnie into the closet, Julie bumped right into her just inside the secret room.

"I thought your weren't coming."

"Oh, shut up and give me one of those lights," said Julie, holding out one of her hands. "Let's get this over with," she said heading into the first tunnel.

"No talking until we get to the first door," whispered Donnie.

Turning on their lights, both girls didn't say a word until they were at the first door.

"Be careful in this next tunnel. It was wet last night, and that was without this storm," said Julie.

Pulling on the latch, Donnie and Julie quietly opened the door and stepped inside the new tunnel.

Julie had been right about the floor of this tunnel. It was not only wet, but also this time it had puddles standing every few feet.

"I don't like this at all," Julie said almost falling.

"Just keep going," said Donnie pushing Julie forward.

Wishing that she hadn't entered these tunnels again, Julie moved ahead, closely followed by Donnie. How foolish she had been to let Donnie talk her into this the first time, but a second time was really foolish.

Rounding one last corner, the girls made their way down the last tunnel leading to the locked door.

Getting that old feeling of doom in her stomach, Donnie suddenly thought about the men from the night before. What if she was wrong and they had entered the tunnel before her and Julie? What if when they opened the door they stood inside?

Maybe Julie had been right when she didn't want to come.

Maybe they should just turn around and go back.

"What's wrong now?" asked Julie, shining her light on Donnie's face.

"I'm not sure we should be here," Donnie answered.

"Now you decide that we shouldn't be here," said Julie almost laughing.

"Remember what you said last night?"

"Like it or not, we are here. Let's find that key, open this door and never ever come back here again," Julie said as she reached up to move the board hiding the key.

"Is this what you're looking for?" came a voice from behind them—a voice both girls had heard many times before….

Chapter 17

"I said, 'Is this what you're looking for?'" repeated the voice behind Donnie and Julie.

Looking at each other for another second, both girls turned to face a figure known quite well by both of them—a figure that now stood blocking the only way out of the tunnel and holding the key that was no longer hidden in its secret place.

How could they have missed his blue eyes earlier in the day at the inn?

Not saying a word, both girls just stared at his blue eyes—the same blue eyes that always seemed to see right into a person's soul; the same blue eyes that Donnie had seen many times in the past several days; the same blue eyes that belonged to the mysterious man in black; and the same blue eyes that had always belonged to Doc Phillips.

"Don't you have anything to say?" asked Doc Phillips.

Still not answering, the girls seemed to be frozen as they just stood staring at him.

"I can't believe that two such meddling girls like you don't have one word to say to me. I bet you'll have plenty to say once you see what's behind that door."

Grabbing both girls, Doc Phillips shoved Donnie and Julie forward to face the still locked door.

"Here, Donnie, take this key. You couldn't wait to see what's hidden in there. Now open that door," said Doc as he shoved a large golden key into Donnie's hand.

Almost in tears now, Donnie reached up and placed the

golden key into a large padlock that hung from the wooden door. Turning it with a loud click, the large lock popped open at once.

"Get out of the way," said Doc Phillips, still holding on tightly to Julie and pushing Donnie out of his way.

Yanking the opened lock from the door, he swung the door open, revealing a large room that was completely dark. Grabbing both girls, Doc led them both through the open door into the darkness.

Donnie and Julie let out a whimper as they heard the wooden door close behind them, wondering where this evil man was leading them in the darkness.

"Keep moving," said the gruff voice as Julie almost fell.

"Please, where are you taking us?" asked Donnie.

The evil man kept dragging the two girls and didn't answer as he just kept moving through the darkness.

"Please, I need to rest," begged Julie.

But the evil man kept moving, not saying a word.

Donnie was sorry that she had ever come back to this place, and she was even sorrier that she had talked Julie into following her. Not another person at the inn knew about the secret room or the tunnels. They wouldn't be missed until morning, and that would be too late.

Donnie knew now that she had trusted the wrong person and wished that Rodney were here to help her, like he had so many times before—first at the bridge, and then at the lighthouse when the old man had attacked her.

Granny Kelly had been right. She had been fighting with Rodney since arriving at the inn a few days ago, trying to deny the fact that he made her heart beat faster when he was near.

Donnie's heart skipped a beat just thinking about Rodney rescuing her from this evil man.

"Step up," said Doc, forcing Donnie to stop thinking about Rodney.

Lifting her feet upward, Donnie soon found that they were being dragged up a staircase.

Where's this man taking them? she thought as they climbed higher and higher.

If she didn't know better, Donnie would swear that they were in the old lighthouse where old man Hank had attacked her earlier in the week. But why would the tunnels lead there?

Stepping onto a landing, Donnie looked upward just for a moment, and that's when she knew for sure that she was in the old Seahorse Lighthouse.

Above her head stood the 30-foot light that was once used to warn ships of the impending dangers that might await them on the rocks below.

Before Donnie could see anything else, the evil man pulled her arm so hard that she nearly fell as they started down another set of stairs. Reaching the bottom of the winding stairs, Donnie, Julie and Doc Phillips entered a passageway that stopped right in front of another locked door.

Producing a second key, Doc Phillips quickly opened the door and shoved both girls inside.

Still in the dark, Donnie and Julie huddled together, waiting for the evil man to make his next move.

Suddenly the room lit up as Doc flipped the light switch by the closed door.

Looking around, Donnie and Julie found that they were standing in the middle of a room filled with wooden chests of various sizes, and from what they could see, most of the chests were filled with gold coins.

"Don't you want to touch it?" asked Doc Phillips.

Donnie and Julie still didn't move. They just kept looking

first at the coins and then at each other.

"Aren't you curious about where these came from and why they are such a secret?"

Pulling Donnie over to a chest, the evil man ran her hand down into a chest, making the coins fall to the floor.

"Don't you love how gold feels falling through your fingers? How about you, Julie? Don't you want to know what real gold feels like? All of this is mine, and I am not about to let you two meddling girls ruin my plans."

Grabbing Donnie and Julie again, Doc Phillips led them both toward two chairs that sat behind a large chest.

Almost throwing both girls on to the chairs, he picked up a small rope from one of the chests and began to tightly tie Donnie and Julie to the chairs.

Donnie wanted to cry, but she didn't want to let Doc Phillips know how scared she really was. She wanted to tell him what she thought of him and his stupid gold, but Donnie didn't want to make him any angrier. Instead she kept quiet, and for her, that was hard. She had never been able to keep her mouth shut and was always getting into trouble because she couldn't.

"That should keep you two from going anywhere for a while," said Doc Phillips as he pulled on the knotted roped that held the girls. "I also know that no one will miss either of you before morning, and by then I will have taken care of you two meddling girls once and for all. I knew when Granny Kelly said you were coming for the summer, Donnie, that you would be nothing but trouble. You had always been a nosey child when I saw you on the island years ago, and I just knew you would be meddling into things that you shouldn't. I tried my best to discourage you, Donnie, from the first time on the bridge. I thought if I could scare you right away, you wouldn't want to stay, but nothing I did made you go home, and the worst part of

it all, you had to drag Julie into this too.

"Now, I have two of you to keep from telling the secret that has been hidden in this lighthouse since the Civil War—a secret that I uncovered five years ago when I first went to the Cedar Key museum looking for some material on this old lighthouse and its part in the Civil War. Material that included 75 chests of golden coins that were supposed to help the Union Army during its stay here at Cedar Key. Only for some reason, the Army had to leave suddenly, and the chests were left behind hidden for many years in the tunnels leading from the lighthouse to the inn.

"I thought that's what you had found yesterday when you were at the museum all afternoon searching through the old records there. I hid down the hall until you left. Then I slipped back into the records room and tried to figure out what you had found. But you had put everything back, and I didn't have any idea what you had found. Then I hurried back to the inn in that awful storm hoping to overhear what you might have found. That's when you saw me at the window and screamed. While you were in the kitchen with Granny Kelly, I slipped into the dining room unnoticed and heard you tell Julie not to tell anyone about the man in black or about any of the strange things that had been happening to you since you had arrived.

"I also figured out that you suspected that the man in black knew Rodney Atwater and that you also thought Terry had been acting strange since you had arrived. That's how I know that no one will miss either of you until morning. You haven't even shared all the strange things going on with Granny Kelly, because you didn't want to worry her.

"So I know at least for tonight that everything is still a secret and I have enough time to take care of you two and the gold as well.

"I also know how foolish I have been to let this key out of my sight, and from now on, no one but me will be the keeper of the key.

"Well, I have things to do," Doc said as he turned off the lights, leaving Donnie and Julie in total darkness again.

Not saying another word, Doc Phillips just opened the door and was gone, leaving the girls alone to wonder what would happen to them when he returned….

Chapter 18

Why had they come back a second time when they had escaped unharmed the night before? Was it the lure of the locked door? Was it just being too stubborn, knowing all along that they shouldn't have ever come back to this place?

How long would it be before they were missed? Maybe days if the hurricane outside of their prison kept raging. How foolish they had been to not tell another person about the secret room or the long maze of tunnels that connected this place with the inn. Now they were in this place all alone, wishing over and over that someone knew that they were here.

Hearing the door lock as Doc Phillips left, Donnie felt a cold chill creep up her spine as his footsteps faded into the distance.

"Are you alright?" she asked Julie, as Donnie tried to see her in the darkness.

"No, I am not alright," answered Julie. "How could I be alright when I am tied up in dark place with a mad man coming back later to take care of us? Why did I ever listen to you a second time and come back to this awful place?"

"I'm sorry that I dragged you into this whole mess," said Donnie, trying to loosen the ropes that held her hands behind her back.

"Not, as sorry as I am."

Not saying another word, both girls just sat in silence, listening as the wind howled outside of their prison, wondering how long they had before the insane Doc Phillips returned.

The longer she sat there, the madder Donnie became. She was a fighter, and no way was she going to let Doc Phillips harm her or Julie.

"Listen to me, Julie. I know all of this looks hopeless, but I am not giving up yet. We have to try and do something before he comes back."

"Do something, how?" asked Julie. "Did you forget that we are both tied to these chairs?" snapped Julie.

"No, but I have a plan if we can get our chairs closer to each other. Listen to my voice in the dark and try to wiggle toward the sound. Once we can touch each other, maybe we can figure out how to untie our hands. Now, move."

Even though Julie thought that Donnie was crazy, thinking that they could move the chairs, she began to wiggle. Donnie kept saying over and over to move this way, and Julie started to scoot her feet on the floor.

Even in the darkness, Donnie was starting to see Julie's chair, and she began to slide her feet on the floor too.

Suddenly their knees touched.

"See I knew we could do it," said Donnie as she stopped moving.

"Now, I need to turn my chair so you can reach my hands," Donnie said as she started to slide her feet and wiggle her chair backwards, moving closer to Julie.

Sliding and wiggling for what seemed like hours, Donnie was starting to get tired, and she still hadn't been able to turn her chair enough so Julie could reach her hands.

Stopping to rest, Donnie was starting to wonder if she would ever be able to turn enough to reach Julie.

As she rested in the darkness, Donnie couldn't get Rodney off her mind. She had been so wrong about him, and now she might never see him again.

No way was she going to let Doc Phillips get away with stealing all that gold or keep her from seeing Rodney again. Donnie started to move the chair, and this time it slid around, almost tipping over. When it came back down on all four legs, the chair had landed right in front of Julie, with Donnie's back to her.

"Okay, Julie, slide this way," said Donnie, wiggling her hands trying to loosen the ropes, as Julie began to move her chair closer to Donnie.

Suddenly Julie could feel Donnie's hands as she turned her chair just a little more.

"I can feel you hands," said Julie in an excited voice.

Stretching as far as she could, Julie began to try to tug on the ropes that held Donnie's hands behind her back. Her wrists stung as the ropes dug into them, but Julie kept trying to reach Donnie.

While Julie pulled on the ropes, they began to loosen. Donnie started moving her wrists, and all at once the ropes on Donnie's wrist let go.

She quickly pulled the ropes from her hands. Pulling again, Donnie started to loosen the ropes that held her to the chair.

"I'm free. I'm free," Donnie yelled as she jumped up.

Hurrying behind Julie, she untied the knotted ropes as fast as she could. In another minute, Julie was free too.

Both girls stood in the darkness, rubbing their stinging wrist and thinking how glad they were to be free, at least from the chairs.

Not wanting to waste any more time, Donnie felt her way over to the door and switched on the light, flooding the dark room with light.

Then she tried the door, hoping it was not locked. Finding that it was still locked, Donnie moved back over by Julie.

Looking around the chest-filled room, Donnie soon realized that the only way out was the locked door. She had been hoping for a window or even another door, but the only way out was locked.

"What do we do now?" asked Julie.

"We need some kind of plan before Doc Phillips comes back, but I don't have any idea what to do," said Donnie as she sat down.

Sitting down by Donnie, Julie didn't say a word. The girls just sat and listened as the storm outside raged on.

"Maybe we should turn off the lights. If Doc Phillips sees them, he will know that we are free," Donnie suddenly said. "Why don't we move over behind that large chest in the corner, and we can at least be hidden when he comes back," said Donnie hurrying, hoping that Doc wouldn't open the door before she could reach the light switch.

Feeling her way in the darkness, Donnie joined Julie behind the chest, trying not to fall on the way.

Sitting against the cold wall of the lighthouse, the girls once again sat in silence, trying now to listen for any movement by the locked door.

Suddenly the wall behind the girls shook. It rumbled so hard that it shook the floor under them. The storm outside was getting worse, and it was trying to blow the walls down around Donnie and Julie.

Moving away from the rumbling walls, Donnie and Julie huddled together in the middle of the room, fearing that at any moment they would be buried forever as the walls of the lighthouse shook harder and harder.

"I'm scared," said Julie as the sound of the wind outside grew louder.

Moving once again, the girls crouched down by the shaking

walls of the lighthouse, covering their head, as they had been taught many years ago in school, and wondering how much longer the walls could take the pounding of the raging wind and rain.

Why did we ever come to this place? both girls thought as the walls above them began to crack. Moving away from the cracking sound, Donnie and Julie both wanted to scream, fearing that they would be buried alive in the lighthouse with its secrets forever....

Chapter 19

Huddling together, Donnie and Julie didn't move as pieces of the rumbling walls fell all around them, just missing the girls within inches.

Then it stopped as quickly as it had begun. No more rumbling, no more wind, just silence.

The girls didn't move. They just stayed huddled together, waiting, hoping that nothing else would fall down around them.

In another few minutes, Donnie and Julie moved. Looking above them into the darkness, the girls decided that the lighthouse was still standing, at least for now.

Moving closer to the wall, where they first heard the rumblings, Donnie and Julie saw a hole, a rather large hole that had just opened up from all the pounding from the storm outside the lighthouse. A hole that seemed to be just the right size to climb through.

Sticking her head through the hole into the pouring rain, Donnie could see the wet ground just on the other side.

We must be in the very bottom of the lighthouse, Donnie thought as she pulled her now soaked head back inside the room.

"Come here," she yelled to Julie. "This is our way out," Donnie yelled again before starting to enter the hole.

Hanging out into the pouring rain, she began to pull the rest of her body through the open hole.

"Push me," said Donnie when she couldn't move another inch through the hole.

Julie pushed as hard as she could, sending Donnie sailing through the hole, causing her to fall right out the other side into the wind and rain.

"Come on," yelled Donnie back into the hole. "I'll help you through once I can see you."

Julie started sliding through the hole as quickly as she could, not wanting to be caught halfway in the hole by the evil Doc Phillips.

Donnie waited by the hole, wanting her to hurry. Seeing Julie's head, Donnie reached in, and with one yank had her pulled through, causing her to land in the same mud hole that Donnie had sat in earlier.

Feeling much safer now, Donnie help Julie stand.

"Which way do we go?" asked Julie, trying to decide which way they should head.

"I am not sure, but I am not going to stand here another minute and wait for Doc Phillips to find us gone," answered Donnie, starting around the side of the lighthouse.

Following behind, Julie could barely stand up as the wind and rain pounded her. Realizing that they must go down the sandy hill to cross the bridge, Donnie led the way.

Not looking back, Donnie ran, hoping that Julie was following. She couldn't remember ever being in such a violent storm. The winds were the strongest she had ever felt, blowing harder and harder as she tried to stay upward.

Julie struggled as she also tried to stay up. Falling several times, she felt the sand on the hill dig right into her legs. Julie knew without looking that she was bleeding. *Please don't let me lose my way*, she thought, trying to see through the sheets of rain that poured in her face.

Then Donnie saw the bridge. Only a few more feet and she would be on her way to the inn. Stopping, Donnie turned to see

if Julie was still behind her, but the rain was falling so hard that she couldn't even see the lighthouse.

Donnie turned and started back up the sandy hillside. She couldn't leave Julie. She had gotten Julie into this, and no way could she leave her behind.

Going uphill was almost impossible, Donnie found as she struggled, fighting the wind and rain. Where was Julie? Why wasn't she coming?

Maybe the demented Doc Phillips had discovered the open hole and come after them. What would she do if he had caught Julie?

"Oh, please let her be safe," Donnie said as she tried to shout over the raging storm.

"Julie, Julie, where are you?" yelled Donnie.

"Here, over here," shouted Julie trying to pull herself up.

"What happened?" Donnie asked as she reached Julie.

"The wind was blowing so hard that I couldn't follow, and I just sat down and cried."

Hooking their arms together, Donnie and Julie started back down the hillside, fighting the wind with every step that they took.

Donnie couldn't decide which was worse, the wind almost knocking them down or the rain that pounded them over and over. Every muscle ached in her body as she forced her way though the storm.

Suddenly Donnie and Julie saw the bridge right in front them, and they rushed to cross it.

Only a little farther, and they would be at the inn—safe at the inn, away from the wind and the rain and letting people know about the crazy Doc Phillips, with his secrets at the Seahorse Lighthouse.

Making it to the other side of the bridge, Donnie and Julie

felt a little better as they hurried up the path toward the inn.

Rounding the corner, the girls started to almost run as they saw the lights from the inn. Only a few more steps and this awful night would be over and Donnie would be seeing the man that made her heart skip whenever he was near.

Starting up the steps leading from the path, Donnie and Julie hurried as they saw a figure waving, knowing that safety was only a few feet away.

Hoping that it was Rodney, Donnie started running up the last few steps. Then stopping, as she suddenly realized that the figure waving wasn't Rodney, or Terry or even Granny Kelly. It was the crazed madman Doc Phillips that stood waiting for her and Julie.

Not moving at first, the girls just stared with disbelief. They were so close. Just a few more feet and they would have been safe.

Laughing as he started down the steps toward the girls, Doc Phillips started to wave again.

Turning and running back down the steps, Donnie and Julie ran back up the path, followed now by the one thing keeping them from the inn, Doc Phillips.

Where could they go? They both knew that they didn't want to go back to the lighthouse again. Running and almost sliding over the edge of the path, Donnie suddenly turned to the right and headed up another path, followed by Julie. A path that went higher and higher as it led the trio farther and farther away from the safety of the inn.

Reaching the top, Donnie and Julie stopped as they realized they were cornered. On one side of them was the ocean below with waves 50 feet high, and coming right at them was the crazed Doc Phillips!

Looking at each other, Donnie and Julie knew they were

trapped. As the wind picked up once again, the girls prepared to meet their fate.

Doc Phillips appeared right in front of them, laughing as he came closer and closer, knowing that they couldn't escape.

"Now once and for all, I am going to take care of you two meddling girls," Doc Phillips yelled as he lunged forward.

Grabbing Donnie and Julie, Doc Phillips started pulling them closer to the edge of the cliff. Struggling, trying not to go over the edge, Donnie and Julie fought with every ounce of strength that they had left.

If they were going over the edge, Doc Phillips wasn't going to have an easy time. Kicking him, Julie almost broke free. Looking into those wild blue eyes, Donnie slipped as he pushed, trying to put her over the edge.

Looking down at the rocks below, maybe for the last time, Donnie wished she had never come to Cedar Key Island….

Chapter 20

Trying to not go over the edge into the ocean below, Donnie and Julie kept fighting Doc Phillips. Pushing them closer and closer to the edge, Doc Phillips knew it was only a matter of time before the girls could no longer hold on. Then his secret would be safe once again.

Suddenly from behind them came the voice of Rodney Atwater.

"Stop, stop," yelled Rodney as he ran up the path behind the fighting trio.

Trying one more time to push the girls over, Doc Phillips turned to see Rodney running toward him.

"I said stop!"

Letting go of the girls, Doc Phillips lunged toward Rodney. Falling to the ground, the two men rolled over and over on the slick rocks, getting closer and closer to the edge of the cliff.

Pinning Rodney down, Doc Phillips started pulling him toward the edge of the cliff. Seeing the danger that Rodney was in, Donnie and Julie jumped in to help.

Pulling hard on Doc Phillips, Donnie and Julie fell backwards, taking him with them and freeing Rodney.

A wild-eyed Doc Phillips jumped up and ran off into the night, leaving the trio to watch as the madman disappeared into the darkness.

Rushing over to Rodney, Donnie and Julie helped him up.

"Are you two alright?" asked Rodney, pulling Donnie into his waiting arms. Not saying a word, Donnie didn't try to pull

away, feeling that this was where she belonged.

"Why was Doc Phillips trying to throw you two into the ocean?" asked Rodney, still holding Donnie close to him.

"He has a secret hidden in the old lighthouse, and we know all about it," said Donnie looking up at Rodney.

"Why didn't you tell someone about what was going on?"

"Because we didn't know who to trust," said Julie.

"We didn't know until tonight that Doc Phillips was the person causing us all kinds of problems."

"You didn't think I was involved, did you?" Rodney asked, letting go of Donnie.

"Let's talk about all of this back at the inn where we aren't standing on the edge of a cliff during a high wind," said Donnie wanting to avoid making Rodney mad.

"You're right. We need to get down from here," said Rodney taking a hold of Donnie's hand.

With Julie in front, the trio started back down the path toward the inn, barely able to see through the heavy rain that seemed to be blowing sideways.

Unable to see very far in front of him, Rodney was starting to wonder if he would ever reach the inn with the two girls. Moving slowly, he held on to Donnie and Julie, trying to stay away from the edge of the path by the ocean.

Finally, the trio reached the bottom of the steps leading up to the inn. Grabbing a hold of the wooden railing, Rodney anchored himself as he tried to pull the girls up on the first step.

"Grab a hold of the railing," he shouted, pulling Donnie up behind him.

Then grabbing Julie, he pulled her up, placing her hand on the railing too.

The three just stood now holding on so tight that their arms

ached, as the wind blew harder and harder, making it impossible to move up or down.

"Hold on and don't let go," shouted Rodney, hoping that the wooden railing would withstand the pounding of the strong winds and rain.

Watching the trio from above, an unseen figure crouched behind the large rocks that stood to one side of the wooden steps. If he were lucky, the three meddlers below would be blown out into the ocean, never to be seen again. Then he could move the chests before someone else found them.

How much longer could they hold on? The wind had to be at least 130 miles an hour now. Why didn't thc ancient wooden railing let go and throw them all out to sea?

He couldn't believe how Donnie and Julie could survive again and again.

If that other meddler, Rodney Atwater, hadn't been there the first night by the bridge, Donnie would not have survived the first attack.

Standing once more, the hidden figure peered down at the still struggling group below, hoping that he wouldn't have to hide much longer.

Then the winds and rain just stopped as the hurricane's eye reached a calm that could last for up to an hour, giving a little relief before continuing.

Donnie, Rodney and Julie stood very still as they waited for another gust of the strong wind to hit them. When nothing came, they let go of the wooden railing,

The figure crouched behind the rocks once again, as he waited to see what the three meddlers were going to do next.

Rodney hugged both girls as he realized that the wind had stopped, and at least for now they were safe.

Not saying a word Donnie, Rodney and Julie turned and

started up the stairs, arm in arm, wanting to reach the inn before the calm storm started up again.

Waiting for the trio to reach the top, the hidden figure prepared to jump. If he could catch them offguard, he could push all three of them back down the stairs before they could react.

Almost smiling now, Donnie, Rodney and Julie at last reached the top of the stairs leading to the inn, knowing that they would all soon be safe inside.

Jumping from behind the rock, Doc Phillips shoved as hard as he could, as he met the unsuspecting trio at the top of the stairs.

Letting go of the girls, Rodney fell as he tried to keep his footing on the rain soaked stairs. Donnie managed to fall onto the path, but Julie tumbled backwards down several steps before she could stop.

Jumping up, Donnie started to run. Doc Phillips followed close behind, knowing if Donnie reached the inn, he was done.

Reaching the steps leading on to the porch of the inn, Donnie tripped as she started upward. Doc Phillips was right behind her.

"I have you now, you little meddler," yelled Doc Phillips as he pulled her down from the porch steps.

Pulling himself up, Rodney ran up the stairs and up the path leading to the inn, hoping that he wasn't too late to help Donnie.

Donnie wasn't about to let the crazed Doc Phillips pin her down. Kicking and shoving as he tried to pull her closer to the bottom of the steps, she tried with every ounce of strength left in her to free herself.

With one last kick, Donnie was free. Jumping up, she ran down the path leading behind the inn, followed closely by Doc Phillips.

As Rodney reached the inn's steps, he saw Doc Phillips just before he disappeared behind the inn.

"Stop," shouted Julie as she ran up behind Rodney.

"Where is Donnie?" asked Julie as Rodney started down the path that led behind the inn.

"I am not sure, but I just saw Doc Phillips headed that way, and I can just about bet that he is chasing Donnie," answered Rodney as he started to run again.

Julie just stood and watched Rodney disappear behind the inn. She wasn't going another step.

"I've had enough," Julie said out loud as she started to climb the steps of the inn.

Behind the inn, Donnie was running for her life. Doc Phillips was right behind her. Once she had made it to the back door of the inn, she found it locked. Of course she couldn't find a window to climb through, since they were all covered with hurricane shutters.

Twice, he had been right behind her, but she had lost him. Where could he be? Where were Rodney and Julie? Had they been hurt when they had fallen? She had to stay alive to let people know about this demented man and his secrets hidden at the Seahorse Lighthouse.

Where could they be? Rodney hadn't seen either Donnie or Doc Phillips since they had disappeared behind the Inn.

Where is that girl? thought Doc Phillips, standing by the back door of the inn.

"Come back here," screamed the crazed Doc Phillips seeing Donnie suddenly crossing the field behind the inn.

Not looking back, Donnie ran. Doc Phillips ran. He had to catch her.

Peering into the darkness, Rodney spotted the two figures as they raced across the field in front of him.

Starting to run now, Rodney knew he had to reach Donnie before Doc Phillips.

Trying to catch her breath, Donnie ran. She ran down another path, not caring where it led, as long as she could get away from the madman running behind her.

Looking behind her once more, Donnie suddenly stepped into a clearing—a clearing that had her trapped. She was on a cliff above the sea for the second time in one night.

Doc Phillips almost laughed as he entered the clearing, seeing that Donnie was trapped. She was all his.

Backing up, Donnie almost slipped as Doc crossed the clearing.

"Stop," yelled Rodney as he too entered the clearing.

Acting like he didn't hear Rodney, Doc Phillips just kept moving.

"I said stop!"

Still not stopping, Doc Phillips lunged at Donnie as hard as he could. He wanted to make sure that this time, Donnie didn't escape.

Seeing what Doc was about to do, Rodney ran faster.

Then Donnie moved. Not a lot, but just enough for Doc Phillips to miss her—just enough to send the madman with the blue eyes over the edge before he could regain his balance.

Running over to the edge of the cliff, Rodney and Donnie looked down into the rocks and sea below. Doc Phillips' body had already disappeared into the raging waves.

Putting his arms around Donnie, Rodney held her for a long time without saying a word.

"Don't you think we need to get back to the inn?" asked Rodney as he let go of Donnie.

Yes, it's time to let everyone know about Doc Phillips' secrets," answered Donnie as she looked at the spot where Doc

Phillips had stood only minutes before.

Realizing how lucky she had been, Donnie didn't say another word. She just took Rodney by the hand and headed back across the field to the inn, knowing that everything was going to be just fine.

Epilogue

Donnie stood on the balcony of her room at the inn, staring out into the ocean, wondering if they would ever find the body of Doc Phillips. It had been almost a year since he had disappeared over the cliff into the ocean, and she still couldn't get that awful night out of her mind.

Down on the beach, she could see Mark, Terry and Julie all taking a morning walk. Julie and Terry were holding hands, watching as Mark stopped to pick up a new shell to put in his bag. They were going to be a family soon. In the year following the death of Doc Phillips, Terry and Julie had discovered how they really felt about each other, and they would be married in the spring.

Donnie had been so wrong about so many things. She had been wrong about Hank, the old man that had knocked her down at the lighthouse. She had been so wrong about him being involved in any of the strange happenings. Hank knew about the treasure, but Doc Phillips had told Hank that he would kill anyone that came near the lighthouse, and that included Granny Kelly, a woman that had been the only real friend that Hank ever really had. When Rodney and Hank argued earlier at the lighthouse, he had admitted to Rodney that he wasn't driving the car that nearly hit Donnie on the bridge when she first came to the inn. But he wouldn't tell who the person was, for fear that he would hurt Granny Kelly.

As for the two men in the tunnels, they turned out to be antique thieves, selling the coins that Doc Phillips had on the

black market. Hank also knew where the police could find these men. They had been arrested before they could leave Cedar Key Island.

The storm was a hurricane, and it's a wonder that she, Rodney and Julie survived to tell anyone about the chests hidden in the Seahorse Lighthouse or about the evil Doc Phillips. Not too many people could run around in a hurricane and live to tell about it.

As for the chests filled with coins, it turns out that they had been hidden in the tunnels between the lighthouse and the inn during the Civil War. When the Union Army took over the inn and the lighthouse, they had built the tunnels leading from the inn to the lighthouse. At first they used the tunnels only as a safe passageway leading the soldiers back and forth unseen from the lighthouse and the inn. Later, when the war was coming to a close, several shipments of the golden coins were placed in the tunnels. When the Union Army left Cedar Key Island near the end of the war, the chests filled with coins were left behind. They were too heavy to transport at the time, and that is where they remained until Doc Phillips accidentally found a secret room behind his closet a few years ago, leading him through the tunnels right to the coins. As to why the Union Army didn't come back for the coins, no one knows. The coins were turned over to the people of Cedar Key Island to decide what to do with them.

Donnie had also been wrong about Rodney Atwater being involved in all the strange things that had happened to her. He just happened to always be near enough to help her, just like when Doc Phillips tried to throw her and Julie off the cliff and into the ocean. He was her knight in shining armor, always there just in the nick of time to rescue her from any danger that she might be facing.

Waving now at the handsome figure of a man coming up the path, Donnie smiled as she thought of the future that she was going to have here—a future spent as the wife of a fisherman and the new kindergarten teacher on Cedar Key Island in the fall.